P9-CDK-179

THE HIDDEN KNIFE

THE HIDDEN KNIFE

MELISSA MARR

NANCY PAULSEN BOOKS

NANCY PAULSEN BOOKS

An imprint of Penguin Random House LLC, New York

Nancy Paulsen Books is a trademark of Penguin Random House LLC.

Visit us online at penguinrandomhouse.com

Library of Congress Cataloging-in-Publication Data
Names: Marr, Melissa, author.
Title: The hidden knife / Melissa Marr.
Description: New York: Nancy Paulsen Books, [2021] | Summary: "After a tragedy, Vicky bands together with new friends to seek justice in dangerous Glass City, where the magical gargoyles are always watching"—Provided by publisher.
Identifiers: LCCN 2020018830 | ISBN 9780525518525 (hardcover) | ISBN 9780525518532 (ebook)
Subjects: CYAC: Gargoyles—Fiction. | Fantasy.
Classification: LCC PZ7.M34788 Hid 2021 | DDC [Fic]—dc23
LC record available at https://lccn.loc.gov/2020018830

Manufactured in Canada
ISBN 9780525518525

3 5 7 9 10 8 6 4 2

Design by Eileen Savage | Text set in Skolar Latin

To Nancy Paulsen, from Bunny Roo to wild horses
and politics and parenthood, you *get* me and my words.
This book exists because you understood what I was trying
to say before I did. Thank you for everything.

THE HIDDEN KNIFE

PROLOGUE

The gargoyles were the first creatures to leave the Netherwhere. They hadn't planned it, and they didn't do it to impress the rest of the things that lived between worlds. They were simply curious.

There was a door. On the other side of it was sky. The air tasted lighter, and the light was gentle. In the Netherwhere, the sky was indigo with streaks of green and purple. Sometimes, there were thick pinks. The new sky was brighter.

One of the eldest gargoyles, a giant-eared wonder called Rupert, stood at the door to the new world and watched as hundreds of his kind took flight. He waited, trying to decide if he wanted to go through the door.

The thought of flying without so much effort was tempting. In the new world's lighter air, even the weightiest among them soared like the faeries could. And as if summoned by the mere thought, one of the faeries darted at Rupert. The faeries' vicious teeth couldn't pierce stone, but that never stopped them from trying. The tiny clack of faery teeth was almost their version of a greeting by now.

Rupert shook the beast off as its little teeth scraped his shoulder. "Stop that."

"All of you?" The faery nodded toward the door. "All go?"

Rupert looked back at the forest. The tree boughs were nearly empty. Maybe they had already left, or maybe they were coming back now. Or later. Time was different to gargoyles. It was forward and backward at once.

"For now," Rupert said.

The faery's wings made a whirring sound, beating faster than anything should rightly move, but that was faeries: always too fast, always too excited; really, they were too much of *everything*.

"We will go, too!" the faery said.

Rupert nodded slowly. He might have said more, but by the time he'd lifted his eyes, the tiny pest was gone. It flew away in a blur of glittering wings and buzzing sounds.

As he watched it go, Rupert understood why some creatures lied. He wished he could lie to the faeries to prevent them from going through the door, but gargoyles *didn't* lie.

Rupert shook his feathered head and flew into the soft blue sky on the other side of the door. As he gazed down at the ground, he saw strange featherless creatures that looked a lot like the faeries but lacked wings. They swarmed all over fields and towns, clustered on boats and atop carriages, and darted in and out of buildings.

Other beings from the Netherwhere were also spilling into this new world. The opening of the gate was hard to resist.

There were new lands, new adventures, and when you lived such a long life, the new was tempting.

Rupert watched it all—kelpies running toward waterways, wee dragonets seeking warm hearths, and faeries hurtling toward forests. The two-legged creatures who were here first stared at the new arrivals, too, sometimes in awe, sometimes in shock.

Rupert would find a purpose here. A reason. A mission.

The tall spires and jagged arches of some of the most splendid buildings here didn't draw his attention. He continued on, feeling the hum of magic, the drawing of wards, the prickle of ley lines.

The lines in the new world—great underearth streaks of energy to use for magic—were tucked under the soil. These ley lines were how the gargoyles saw future things and now things. They were particularly strong here, and Rupert's mind felt muddled.

He flew toward one of the plainest buildings he'd seen in this world, knowing that the plainest exterior was often a disguise for the most interesting discoveries. He would make a nest here, a place to return and watch this new world.

Rupert settled down on the ledge, and those gargoyles that followed his leadership came in for a landing all around him. He stretched his wings wide and stared back at the beings on the ground, who were craning their necks to see him. They opened their mouths, but nothing they said aloud made sense. Many of their thoughts were noise, but Rupert pulled a taffy-like piece of energy from the ley line and began to learn their language.

"What are you?" he asked.

The creatures swarmed at first. Then one of them met his gaze and said, "I am Tik, a human, a *boy*. A student here at the school."

The human boy creature was a spindly thing. A long twist of hair was bound at the back of his head, reminding Rupert of a kelpie's tail. His skin was dark, like the gargoyles', as well.

Tik held a metal stick that was as pointed as Rupert's own beak, but long and thin. Rupert stared at it curiously.

"It's a sword. I'm training to serve the Glass Queen."

"Why?"

Then Tik laughed. It was a happy noise, especially for a creature determined to serve a queen. "You're a strange . . . What *are* you?"

"Gargoyle. From the Netherwhere."

"Nightshade! Sweeney! Come here." Tik waved to a few other small humans. When they reached him, he said, "The astronomers were right. The World Door opened."

"Not *the* World Door. Just a door between *your* world and the Netherwhere," Rupert corrected, peering at the other humans.

Nightshade was a keen one, and he had the smell of the Netherwhere already on him. Sweeney had a strange, rounder shape; he seemed soft where Nightshade and Tik were narrow.

"Did everything come through?" Nightshade asked with more than a touch of fear in his voice.

Rupert eyed him with more interest. "The faeries did. Kelpies . . ."

4

Nightshade's eyes widened, but he said nothing.

"Kelpies?" Sweeney asked.

"Water horses," Nightshade whispered.

Rupert explained: "Four-legged beasts that breathe water and land air. Hide the color of blue milk. Carnivorous, messy things. They will be a problem for your kind. Our sort is not meat, but you are . . . *all* meat and bone."

"Yes. The queen will need to know," Tik said. "I'll tell the headmaster and request a meeting with Her Majesty to share what you learn."

"If *he* will let us meet her," Sweeney muttered.

Rupert looked at the boys. He was not sure what a headmaster was, or who served whom here. What he did know was that the door opening would lead to changes—and these young creatures might be in peril. Gargoyles were not left this defenseless when they were young.

Sweeney walked away to join a female human who was swinging her pointy sword-thing at a group of boys. The girl was dark-eyed and dark-haired. Her arms had thin white lines where skin had bled and healed again. And she was as tall and strong as the boys, who were all trying to take her weapon.

Rupert stretched his clawed feet out, scratching the ledge in the process, and watched the girl laugh as she unarmed each boy. "Tell me of this queen," the gargoyle said.

Young Tik was eager to do so; his lips curved in a curious expression that Rupert understood meant happiness, because of the words that followed.

"She's only a few years older than us, but already she's a queen. She's going to create a new empire, rule the world, and if we're good enough, we can serve her." Tik shoved his shoulders back. "She's called Evangeline . . . like an avenging angel."

"Angel?"

"You know. Winged creatures from another world."

Rupert paused. "A gargoyle. Your queen is a gargoyle?"

Tik laughed again. "No. She's a human like me, but wiser and kinder and better in all ways. She looks after us and will protect our borders. She is our guardian."

Tik sounded like he believed his own words, but Nightshade's expression said that he wasn't so sure he agreed with Tik.

These humans would all need watching over, and the gargoyles were the right ones to do it. Rupert could already see enough of the future to know that their queen was not to be trusted.

Looking after others wasn't just about borders, but about adding good to the world—any world.

Yes, it felt right to be here. It had been too long since he'd had a proper mission. Watching over these featherless creatures so he could help when this queen of theirs became trouble was a worthy reason to stay.

Part I

TWENTY YEARS LATER . . .

CHAPTER 1

◆—————◇—————◆

Vicky

H it me!" her mum said. Kathleen Wardrop sounded frustrated, which was unusual when they had weapons in hand, but Vicky's sister Lizzie was being contrary.

They were all in the training room—in what was intended to be the house's ballroom, but really balls weren't quite the things for the Wardrop family. Instead, twelve-year-old Vicky; her older sister, Lizzie; and baby sister, Alice, went there every day to train with their mother, Kathleen Wardrop. Sometimes Lizzie begged off and spent a few hours playing with Alice so Vicky could do ward training. Today, though, was swords. Lizzie was required to do some sword practice at least two times a week, no matter how much she fussed.

"I *did* hit you," Lizzie said, voice slightly muffled by the fencing mask she wore. It made her sound older, stranger. "I touched the tip of my sword to your arm."

Their mother, who did not wear a mask when she trained,

repeated a frequent objection: "That is not a *hit*. If they come for you—"

"But—"

"You need to protect yourself and your sisters," their mum said.

"If you were an actual enemy—"

"Trust no one, Lizzie. No one but your sisters." Their mother sounded grave. "Remember, anyone can betray you."

"Not you," Lizzie pointed out. She stood, almost as tall as their mother, with her shoulders back. "You would die for us. Poppa, too."

"We would." Their mother hugged Lizzie. "But when anyone stands before you with a drawn weapon, you do not *tap* them. You fight."

"Yes, Mother," Lizzie said. She always agreed, but for reasons that Vicky couldn't understand, Lizzie did not like to fight. She was kind in ways that Vicky found confusing, gifted in household affairs, and seemingly unable to fight.

Lizzie left the center of the floor, where they practiced, and headed to the wall racks where swords, staffs, and other weapons hung.

Their mum motioned to Vicky. "Next."

"Ready!" Vicky was prancing like a newborn kelpie on rough waves. Sword time was one of the best parts of the day. Well, to *her* it was.

Vicky bowed to her mother and began to circle her, seeking an opening. She made a few strikes that weren't likely to land, but the openings were there. Ignoring openings was silly.

Within a few moments, the room seemed to fade. The sound of feet on the tiled floor, the clank and slide of steel on steel, the steady exhales as Vicky and her mother fought: only these remained. The rest was gone. Vicky no longer heard the chatter from her baby sister or the soft humming as her elder sister watched. This was what sword fighting was. It made the world vanish, like a fast ballet where each movement was like leaping into the air, and each response was the difference between landing to applause or flopping on the stage like a distressed fish.

Eventually, Vicky's blade made contact with her mother's left side. If Vicky's sword had been sharp, she'd have left a slice on her mum's ribs, but they only practiced with blunted swords.

"Excellent, Vicky Love," her mother said. "Again."

And so they went for the next hour.

Finally, Vicky felt as if her muscles were unable to continue. They'd fought with speed—not drills, not corrections—simply full-speed swords flashing and clattering. It was both one of the hardest things her mother asked her to do and one of the most exciting. She was going to need to nap and curl up with a good book afterward.

"Lizzie?" her mother called. "Your sister is tired. Will you fight now, or will I make Vicky continue?"

To some, Vicky supposed, their mother's tactics might seem cruel, but Kathleen had once guarded the Glass Queen herself. Vicky was sure that the habit of being prepared for disasters was hard to quit; at least that was what Poppa said.

Lizzie sighed. "Fine. I'll never be as good as Vicky, but—"

"You can be good enough to be safe," their mother reminded her sharply. "That's all you need."

Then she glanced at Vicky. "And you might get good enough at proper manners to pass for a nice young lady."

"Doubtful," Lizzie said with a grin.

"Dou'ful!" Alice cheered and clapped. "Dou'ful Vicky!"

Vicky smiled at her sisters as she tugged off her fencing mask. They were all so different. Even though Alice was still a tiny thing, she was already a person of her own. She laughed most of the time but could also throw a good tantrum. Alice, when she was grown, would have a temper that made Vicky and Lizzie seem positively angelic.

"Play with Alice while Lizzie trains," her mother said.

Lizzie, practical like their father, added, "Perhaps fix a few sandwiches—with vegetables. Lunch."

Her mother sighed, glanced at the wall clock in the far end of the room, and nodded. Her voice was light when she said, "Fine. I suppose we all must *eat*, too." She looked at Lizzie. "Thank you, dearest. I do forget, don't I?"

Alice, however, plopped on the floor. "No veg'bulls! Have carrots!"

"Of course, sweetling, no vegetables for you." Their mum scooped Alice into her arms, without so much as touching the youngest Wardrop with her dull-edged sword, and handed her to Vicky. "Alice will have carrots instead of vegetables."

Lizzie and Vicky shook their heads, but that was that. They

would pretend that carrots weren't *actually* a vegetable to keep Alice's temper at bay.

LATER, WHEN THEY'D had their sandwiches—which their father had already made for them—Vicky and Alice sat against the wall of the ballroom. Lizzie and their mother were going over defenses with a sword and dagger.

The room was high-ceilinged, and there were beautiful windows up high that let in light—and the occasional gargoyle.

"Water?" Alice asked.

Vicky shook her head and whispered, "No. Mama says I can't make a lake inside again."

"Gargle story," Alice ordered.

So Vicky started a gargoyle story: "The gargoyles were the first to leave the Netherwhere. A door in the sky opened, and they came to our world."

Everyone knew this story, but Alice loved hearing it over and over.

"They weren't alone," Vicky continued. "The faeries came, and the kelpies, too."

"Gargles best."

Vicky nodded. "Yes, they're our friends."

"Kelpies bite," her sister pronounced with a scowl.

"Yes, and faeries do, too." Vicky wasn't sure about the drag-onets, though. They were often nothing but fading puffs of smoke by the time people even noticed them.

One of the family's gargoyles flew into the ballroom and

winked at her, as if he'd heard her talking about them. The clatter of stone wings should have been loud, but gargoyles moved silently. Whatever magic made them—and the tiny biting faeries and strangely adorable dragonets—didn't always make sense.

Alice blew the gargoyle a kiss, and Vicky waved at him.

Rupert nodded at them but went on to land near their mother. Gargoyles were faithful to those they selected. This one had followed Vicky's mother home from school years ago. He and the other Wardrop gargoyles patrolled like soldiers, carrying messages to Kathleen Wardrop. Kathleen relied upon them to help keep her family safe. With wards, with gates, with swords, and with spies, the Wardrop children were as protected as could possibly be. Vicky, despite all the training and drills for Incidents, could not imagine that there was any possible way that they would ever be in danger.

CHAPTER 2

CRupert

Time was confusing when creatures aged quickly. This was a thing Rupert had learned when he first came through the door. Humans were around for only a blink. They didn't see the future, although some could use ley lines in other ways.

Kat could. Her offspring could.

A minute ago, Kathleen—*Kat*—was small. Somehow, this child of hers was that same size already. *Vicky Love.* That was the girl's name. She was a small thing who looked almost like Kat made young again, but Kathleen was adult-human-sized.

Some things were changeless, though. Greed. Secrets. Rulers who stole lands that weren't theirs and overtaxed people. A queen who forgot that she was meant to serve the people.

Rupert thought about Kathleen when she was still small. When he'd first met her, she was part of a group of friends: Sweeney, Nightshade, Tik, and Kat. They would have done well to stay that way, but it was not to be . . .

"Do you suppose she means to force me to be her guard?" said

the small human girl Kathleen, who was half the size of now. She'd been trying hard to jab her sword into Tik.

Rupert perched in a rafter, watching them. It was what gargoyles did. They watched. They learned. They created small ripples of change.

"It's an honor to guard the queen, Kat."

The girl made a sound like a kelpie snorting and jabbed Tik with her sword.

The boy did not notice that she was also sliding her feet in patterns that pulled ley line energy into the stone-walled room where they stabbed and slashed, danced and dodged.

"I don't want to be a Raven," Kat announced. "I don't want to live in the queen's court. I want a family. I think I had one once, Tik. People loved me."

"We love you!" Albert Sweeney said, looking up from his books. He nudged Nightshade, glared at Tik, and prompted them, "Right?"

They all nodded.

And then Tik flopped to the floor, bound by the wards that Kathleen had drawn while she was fencing. He rolled around, trying to knock into Kat's legs.

"That's why she wants you, Kat," Nightshade said in a fond voice, pointing at Tik. "You're terrifying. The creatures that have come over here are rarely as frightening as you."

Kat made a gesture that freed Tik and sat on the floor next to where Nightshade and Sweeney were studying. "What about what I want?"

None of the friends had replied.

Rupert still wished he could have kept her safe from that day forward. Of all the children at the school, Kat had been special to the queen, and that put her in great peril. There was no way Rupert could steal her away to his world and hide her. He'd taken her to visit the Netherwhere, though.

Rupert swore he'd keep shaping the future as best he could for her, for her children, and help them overcome their fates if he could. Give them knowledge. Give them love. Give them hopes. That was how ripples in time were made. Little moves. Big results.

CHAPTER 3

◇———◇———◇

Algernon

The smoke filtering through the floorboards into the kitchen wasn't alarming, not truly. Neither was Algernon's father's muffled cry from the basement laboratory.

"Masks!" Algernon called out to his brother and all the boys.

If they were in true trouble, the house gargoyles would have swooped into the room by now. It was just another day at Nightshade Manor. However, it was a rule, one well worth obeying, to keep masks within a few yards at all times. Algernon slipped on the birdlike mask. The filters on either side of the beak kept them from inhaling poisonous gases.

"*Mask,*" Algernon again ordered one of the slower boys. Sometimes he was shocked that any of the thieves his father adopted survived. Too many of them lacked the sense that the gods gave a turnip.

"You'll need to train this lot up when I'm gone." Algernon told his brother, Alistair, gesturing toward the five ragged young thieves who'd been slurping soup at the table before the cry from the lab interrupted their meal.

He looked at the boys and stressed, "'Masks on' is an order that you obey the very moment it's said. Before that, if you can."

"Eh," Alistair said with a shrug. "There's always more kids if these are too daft to live."

"Hey!" a few of the boys complained.

Alistair was, by far, the more relaxed of the two Nightshade brothers. As the younger brother, he didn't have to worry about a predetermined future. As long as Algernon didn't fail, Alistair would be free to live his own life. He was just the spare son, the extra one born in case Algernon died.

"Windows!" Master Nightshade shouted as he came bursting through the door. His heavy leather apron flapped like a skirt, and soot from his unsuccessful experiment clung to him. It made his already dark skin seem like shadows.

Four of the five thieves ran to open windows. One of the thieves, London, stared at the chaos. He had put on his own mask but seemed unbothered by the apparent fire and toxic smoke now billowing up the stairs from the lab.

One whispered in awe, "Your father's a madman."

Algernon couldn't argue with that. His father, Aloysius Nightshade, was a master alchemist who had spent his entire life in service to the queen. Lately, it seemed too many of the things he was working on resulted in sudden clouds of smoke and fumes—and repeated calls for the boys to put on their masks.

"London!" the potion maker snapped. "Get to it, boy."

London nodded and began to help. Fortunately, the house was on a country estate, so the poisonous smoke wasn't going to kill any neighbors. Algernon's father wasn't a murderer; he'd said so frequently. He'd never harmed a soul on purpose. His tinctures, elixirs, and ointments did. He, himself, was simply the man who made them.

"Did they all have masks?"

"They did." Algernon looked over to see his father scanning the kitchen floor in search of unconscious boys. "But you'll need to buy more masks if you bring home anyone else."

"Right. Right. Good." His father nodded in that way that made it clear that he hadn't actually heard what Algernon said.

"Father!"

"Mmm?"

"Masks. More. Order them." Algernon spoke in the style he'd learned was useful in dealing with his father when an experiment was all-consuming.

"Oh. Are these masks bad?"

Algernon sighed at having to explain things as if his father were a child. "No. These work. However, we have exactly enough masks for your orphans. Unless one leaves or dies, we need more masks if any more thieves are coming home."

For a moment, Master Nightshade straightened himself in a remarkable imitation of a grown-up and announced, "I only have as many guests as we have masks."

"Until you bring another thief home," Algernon pointed out.

His father waved his hand as if brushing the words away.

"What if one breaks? What if one gets lost?" It was suddenly more than Algernon could manage. None of the staff lasted very long, so running the household fell to him. He was sick of minding his forgetful father. Algernon's voice grew louder. "You need to buy more masks—or hire a new housekeeper to manage all of it."

Just then, the thieves came tumbling back into the kitchen. They were an odd sight, with their masks making them appear as some sort of bird-person hybrids.

"Well, then," the alchemist announced. The hair he hadn't burned off yet stood out in patches. "I suspect that was not the right mixture, eh, children?"

Several of the boys laughed. Algernon exchanged a look with his brother. That joke had gone stale for them years ago.

"An extra helping of whichever meal you choose if you clean the lab," Master Nightside said. "Who wants it?"

Three of the boys said, "Me."

"Keep those masks on, sons. Get gloves, too." He wagged a finger at them. "Nasty stuff down there. Wouldn't do to die before you can get that extra food. Wouldn't do at all."

Algernon shook his head. It wasn't as if the thieves were at any more risk working here than they were living on the streets, but it still bothered him. He and his brother were never asked to clean up the results of experiments—successful or otherwise.

The thieves left with his father, and Algernon was alone with his brother in the giant kitchen.

Alistair shuffled over to stand beside him. "You know I'll take care of the boys when you go. I can watch out for all of us."

"I hate that I have to go to that school at all," Algernon said. "I should have another year."

It wasn't just leaving his brother and the boys. He wasn't ready to start training to create simmering toxins for mischief, murders, or madness. He'd always known that he'd start the Corvus School for the Artfully Inclined the year of his thirteenth birthday, and he'd dreaded it. Somehow, though, he was having to go early—his twelfth birthday had only just passed.

"I don't want to be a killer," Algernon admitted.

"Alchemists aren't killers," Alistair said, parroting the words they'd heard so often.

"Of course," Algernon agreed in response to the lie. He was attending a school to learn to make potions and elixirs that ended lives, that injured or controlled those who defied the queen. He was training to kill at a distance.

And he was terrified.

But there was nothing to be done about it. There had been a Nightshade as the queen's chief poisoner as long as the queen's family had held the throne. They were there before the queen herself, and they would continue to serve long after she was gone. Algernon would be the next one. Like his father and grandfather, he would learn all that the queen required, and one day, when he was good enough, he'd concoct a poison that the *existing* Master Nightshade would drink.

That was the goal. That was tradition—and it was one he wanted to end.

CHAPTER 4

◆———◆———◆

Algernon

Alistair popped his head into the dusty library. "I'm getting wax plugs for our ears, and then we can go."

Algernon nodded and read the list of ingredients yet again. He wasn't sure what it was for, but he was trying to figure it out.

Fresh-cut cress
S̶i̶x̶ Eight jars of mud from the bank
Three leaves from vegetable lamb plant
Sheep leavings
Foxglove
Strips of the red willow
Death caps (stalk, cap, root bulb)
Fool's funnel (stalk and cap)

At the bottom of the paper, in hastily scratched letters was a postscript:

Algernon,
Remember to TAKE THIEVES with you.

A. N.

The initials were large swooping letters, with swirls that branched off from them like wings. The alchemist did not sign his notes any other way. It was as if he were unable to remember that he was writing to his *children* rather than strangers or associates.

Algernon folded up his father's note and shoved it into his trouser pocket. He wasn't sure what his father was making, and Master Nightshade wasn't around to ask.

"Ready?" Alistair asked as they met in the hallway.

They both glanced toward the doorway that led to their father's laboratory. Every so often, sound would filter up to them. Sometimes it was muttered curses, and occasionally it was a raucous cry of victory. Today it was a mix of both.

After a moment, Algernon nodded to his brother, and they went out onto the grounds. The hedges were, like most things at Nightshade Manor, untended and wild. The potion garden was the one exception to the general disrepair of the estate. It was kept tidy, but the lawn, the orchard, and the hedge maze were all unkempt.

They entered the woods as they had countless times before, warily but without unnecessary pause. These adventures in foraging weren't any more dangerous than sleeping in a house with thieves and toxic fumes. Being a Nightshade meant that danger was unavoidable and death was always possible.

That was why there were *two* sons.

24

The Nightshade brothers were only a few steps into the shadowed path under the trees when a gargoyle swooped down over their heads. The mechanics of flying stone always struck Algernon as being wrong. He could understand the basics of alchemy and poisons. That was not so different from cooking. Wards made good sense, too. That wasn't much more than words becoming actions. Astrology was equally sound. A combination of charts, planetary placement at key moments, and a dash of unpredictability . . . really, it was akin to reading maps while at sea.

Flying rocks, however, confounded him. Rocks were heavy; flight required lightness. Birds were hollow-boned and covered in feathers. They were aerodynamic, too, shaped like living projectiles to hurtle through the air. It was logical that birds could fly. Gargoyles shouldn't fly.

"Menace!" Alistair snapped at the creature as it circled them again.

Algernon bit back a laugh. Gargoyles liked his brother, which both irritated and confused Alistair. They liked to nest near him, and when they molted, their falling feathers were *not* light. More than once, a stone feather had thwacked Alistair suddenly.

The gargoyle that was following them drifted in a surprisingly graceful circle over their heads. Its grim-looking mouth curved in a smile, and for a split second, it seemed to give Algernon a cheeky wink before zipping away.

"Someday I'm going to find a way to become invisible to gargoyles," Alistair muttered as he warily scanned the sky.

"Not likely," Algernon said.

His brother let out a surly grunt, but he didn't argue. They'd had this discussion several times. Outsmarting a gargoyle when it wanted to track you was as likely as resisting a potion by sheer willpower.

Science was absolute.

Gargoyles were impossible to avoid if they had their minds set on pursuit. There had even been a move to argue that all gargoyles ought to be either eliminated or returned to the Netherwhere—as if enforcing that nonsense were even *possible*. They watched. They sometimes stalked. Gargoyles, however, did not take commands.

"Why me?" Alistair asked the stony beast as it swooped by again, so close that the wind from its wings made them stumble. "Argh!"

Algernon laughed. He didn't mean to, but the almost growl that his brother aimed at the gargoyles was funny.

"It's not funny!"

"It *is* funny, Ali." Algernon nudged his brother. When Alistair only grunted in reply, he nudged him again. "If you find the lamb pod first, I'll climb it."

Alistair snorted. "You like climbing. That's not a *loss* on your side."

Algernon grinned. "Fine. Whoever finds it first gets to climb it. You get a chance to climb this time."

"And the loser has to collect the droppings," Alistair amended.

They both grimaced. No one liked scooping up sheep poop.

The ingredients that went into potions included nasty things as well as unexpected ones. The lamb pods, for example, were unexpected in good ways. They had thick vines with leaves that curled and layered where the vine connected to the central stem. There, between stem and vine, the layered leaves formed oblong pods. Inside the pods were tiny lambs. They grew there as if they were inside the bellies of mother sheep.

No one understood how or why the plants gave birth to lambs, but the vegetable lamb plants were protected on the queen's order—as were the lambs. If they grew in your area, a good fence was critical. Cute lambs quickly turned into hungry sheep.

"Do you know what he's working on?" Alistair asked as they walked.

"No." Algernon had been going over the list, as he always did, trying to answer that very thing. Sometimes their father's lists were for a specific project, and sometimes he simply needed stores restocked.

Algernon paused to scoop up a few unicorn beetles when he saw them noshing on fallen plums. They were hard to find, so he gathered them when he could.

He also scooped up a few plums—watching for faeries, just in case. Rows of sharp, pointed teeth lined the faeries' mouths like miniature needles. A bite from an angry faery could result in weeks of sickness.

When they heard a loud shriek and saw something sail by them, Algernon braced for faeries. He thought it was about to become a very unpleasant day. He stepped in front of his brother so if there was a faery bite, it would be on him.

But the noise was followed by a *laugh*, and another blur

followed the first. No wings. No swirl of color. No deadly teeth. The blur was mud that was being tossed by three girls.

Quickly, Algernon pulled his brother into a hedge so the girls didn't see them.

"Who are they?" Alistair whispered.

Algernon stared at the girls. He'd never been around any girls, and he was nervous at seeing them.

His father brought home only boy thieves, and Algernon had only the vaguest of memories of his mother. The housekeepers were usually women, but they were older than his father and rarely talked.

As quietly as he could, Algernon said, "Back up."

Alistair didn't argue. He frowned, but he didn't object aloud. He was used to following.

And for a moment, Algernon thought everything was fine. There were strangers in the woods, but they weren't doing anything bad. He could ignore them. The only other choice was to go back to the manor and interrupt his father. No one wanted that.

But then the woman with the girls lifted her head. She looked right at him, and Algernon was certain that he'd rather that they blunder into an entire nest of faeries than her. He *knew* her.

Algernon grabbed Alistair's arm, turned, and walked away so quickly that they both stumbled several times. Once they were far enough away that the woman couldn't see them, Algernon paused.

"There are girls in the woods," Alistair whispered. "*Our* woods."

Algernon nodded. He wanted to tell his brother to shut up, to pretend that they hadn't seen the girls and their mother. He remembered her.

One morning about three years ago, she'd been in the gardens right before dawn, talking with his father.

While his father went inside, Algernon watched the woman. She had moved to stand with her back to the wall of the garden, tucked in so close that the shadows seemed to swallow her. Her attention flitted over the garden. Briefly, it seemed to pause and hover over him.

Algernon knew she'd seen him when she smiled and whispered, "Not a bad job of spying for one so young."

Then his father had returned and handed her a bag, with what Algernon knew came from his private stores. Whoever this woman was, his father was risking everything to help her.

"I saw nothing today," Algernon said firmly. "Neither did you."

Alistair jerked his gaze from the trees and stared at him. "What? They were right here."

"No one was in the woods, Ali."

"But—"

"No one," Algernon repeated. "You saw nothing."

"I don't understand."

"If anyone was here, they were people our father trusts. That means we must, too." He tugged Alistair's arm again. "Come on. We still need to find the death caps."

After a moment, his brother nodded.

CHAPTER 5

❖——❖——❖

Vicky

Vicky was standing in Glass City with her mother. Just the two of them. Their carriage had dropped them at the edge of the city center, where no vehicles were allowed. She stared at the heart of the city in awe.

The streets spiraled out from the Glass Castle, the queen's main residence. Towers pierced the sky, and the Glass Castle was so immense that flying buttresses were essential for the structure to keep from collapsing. The buttresses were not glass, though. Nothing in the castle, aside from the windows, was actually made of glass. It was simply, like so many things, named for their queen.

Queen Evangeline, the self-named Glass Queen, was said to be like glass: delicate and pure. She had only her Ravens to protect her. She said that she was transparent like the most refined glass.

None of that was what Vicky's parents said about the queen. They did not say ugly things about the queen, but they had often reminded Vicky and her sisters that the queen could no longer be trusted. She was *not* transparent—even if she may have started out that way.

"Do you think we'll see the queen?" Vicky asked her mother.

"No."

"We might." Vicky looked at the topmost floor of the highest tower of the castle.

Her mother smiled tightly. "I wouldn't bring you this close to the castle if she were in it. I checked before we came."

Vicky hid a sigh. She'd hoped that she might at least get a glimpse of the queen. She could do a lot more, *if* her mother would agree to it. If her mother wanted to do so, she could even introduce her to the queen. They could go to court and stand in the middle of the highest-ranked citizens in the empire, and Vicky could be *presented* to Queen Evangeline.

"Where are we going?" Vicky asked as she followed her mother.

"A shop you'll like," her mother offered.

"Where?"

"It's a surprise." Her mother smiled and led them deeper into the maze that was the city.

Coming here was an excellent birthday present—even if it did mean having to wear a corset. Until now, Vicky had avoided corsets, but she had turned twelve.

She imagined the constricting thing was not so different from a swamp serpent, squeezing her from hip to armpit, making movement difficult. Vicky took a few very shallow breaths to try to fill up her lungs and wondered how grown-up women managed to accomplish anything while wearing corsets. Maybe—like swords and magic—it got easier with practice.

"Vicky Love? Is all well?" her mother asked gently. Like most of the things her mother said, there were a dozen thoughts and questions in only a few words.

What her mother *meant* was "Did you see a threat?"

"All fine," Vicky said. Coming here was a rare occasion, but Vicky knew enough to be even more alert than usual in the city.

It was hard for Vicky to believe that her mother had once been a Raven, one of the secret elite servants to the Glass Queen herself. Her mother didn't talk about the things she once did for the queen, but she'd said enough that Vicky knew it was dangerous. Now the family stayed away from society, from cities, from everything.

"Did you see something?" her mother pressed.

"No. It's just the corset," she said just as quietly as her mother had spoken. "I'm not used to it yet."

Mama's mouth curled slightly into an almost laugh. "Beastly things, corsets."

Aside from the corset, boots that made her feel like she was balancing her whole body on her tiptoes, and an awkward, stiff dress, Vicky felt good. The city drowned her senses . . . or maybe it was the number of Netherwhere creatures that had taken up residence here.

The most obvious of the beings were the gargoyles. In the country, there were only a few gargoyles. Here, the sky was filled with them. As they leaped from their perches and soared overhead, their shadows fell onto the stone streets, and the entire city was punctuated by the rhythmic sounds of the winged ones.

Even without the gargoyles, Glass City would have been overwhelming. There were market stalls and shops, strangers selling candied fruits and dried meats from their carts, and a dancing girl who moved so quickly that there was no doubt that she *wasn't* wearing a corset. The noise and the smells were enough that Vicky felt dizzy from it.

Or maybe that was the corset.

"Stay near me," her mother reminded Vicky, for what was surely the twentieth time that day.

Vicky didn't point out that she *was* near.

"Girl-beast." One of the gargoyles met her eyes. Most people said that the gargoyles couldn't speak to you unless you were the master of the house, but Vicky understood them. All of them. The crashes, grating, and shrieks that were language to gargoyles sounded as clear as human speech to Vicky.

"Girl-beast," another repeated.

"Ward girl," added a third. This one settled its wings, drawing her attention. He looked familiar.

Vicky studied him. His wing tips extended over his shoulders like the points of a high-collared cloak, giving the gargoyle a regal appearance. So, too, did his sharply hooked nose and almost-human hands. If Vicky had drawn what she imagined a gargoyle king to be, it would be this one. She had privately named him Kingly.

"Kingly," she thought in his direction.

He nodded at her, and she wasn't sure what to do. Why were the gargoyles suddenly trying so hard to get her attention?

Kingly smiled and said only, "Ripples."

"They seem to be screeching a lot today," her mother murmured.

Kingly watched, and Vicky was tempted to wave at him—or ask what *sort* of ripples he meant. In water? In magic? What was he trying to tell her?

"Gargoyles are trustworthy, but you must get in the habit of not staring at them," her mother said. "One day you'll have secrets, Vicky Love, and when you do, you'll need to hide them from *everyone*. The gargoyles cannot read your thoughts unless you meet their eyes."

Vicky couldn't imagine any secret so large that the gargoyles would care. But now that she was twelve, perhaps that was all about to change.

CHAPTER 6

◆ ◇ ◆

Rupert

Rupert tried to divide his watching hours between his humans. Mostly he watched over Vicky, the girl who looked like Kat, and the Nightshade boys. He still visited the ones he'd first met, especially Tik. The boy with the sword had grown into a man who still hoped the queen would save them all, even though his friends had their doubts.

Rupert flew into an upper window at Corvus and descended levels until he reached the room where Tik practiced with his sword. All that had changed there was that the sword and the boy were bigger now. And Tik called himself Meister Tik these days.

And perhaps Tik was safer, finally, living here at the school.

"Rupert!" Tik said irritably as the gargoyle came to rest on the ground too close to where he was swinging his sword.

"You know sitting there is a bad idea," Tik complained, even though he was always able to stop the blade a feather from Rupert's head. "I could injure you."

"You are good with swords, and I treasure the few cracks

Kat gave me over the years. Why would I mind your scratches or cracks?" Rupert stared at him. Humans were strange. If Rupert had been in danger, he wouldn't have landed there.

"What if I hadn't stopped?"

"But you *do* stop." Rupert tilted his head at Tik. He shouldn't find this funny, but he did. He had been doing this since the second time they met. "Kat stops faster."

"Wardrop?"

"Are there other Kats?" Rupert filed through the creatures he'd learned. "Yes. Of course. Lions. Cougars. Tigers. Bear? No. Not bear. Bear is different. Kat looks nothing like a bear."

"Have you seen Kat?"

"Yes. You have, too. You knew her before I came, Tik." Rupert paused, thinking about before and now and later.

Tik crouched down so they were skin to stone. "Is she hurt? *Now?* Does she need me?"

Hurt was a strange thing, too. Hurt? In her heart? In her form? In the now? In the later?

"She is in the city," Rupert said. Then he warned Tik, "When bad things come, guard Kat's child."

And then Rupert was gone, or perhaps Tik was. All Rupert could say for certain was that he turned his head and found that time had passed, and he was alone in a room of swords, without Tik.

CHAPTER 7

◆————◆————◆

Algernon

Algernon Nightshade ducked to avoid being seen as he crept past the open door where the thieves slept. There was always someone awake, but at night, the boys kept to their part of the house, as if trying to avoid attention.

No one—including Algernon—understood why his father brought home the thieves he found in the streets of Glass City. He simply did, and had always done so. And all considered, the ragged boys were the least difficult part of life in Nightshade Manor. Often, they became more like cousins than strangers, which made it hard when they left.

And they *always* left. One day, they'd simply vanish. Algernon had stopped trying to figure out a pattern.

"Sneaking out again?"

Algernon raised his umbrella like a weapon as he turned to scowl at the speaker.

"London! I . . . Perhaps." Algernon didn't have the skill to lie to any of the thieves.

London grinned. "Want company?"

"It's dangerous where I'm going."

"Truly?" London extended an arm that was covered with scars and some red, raised lines. "I have more new scars working for *him* than from lifting baubles in Glass City."

"I need a thieves' oath if you come," Algernon said. "You swear to tell no one where I go."

"And what do I get?"

Algernon shrugged. "What do you want?"

"You'll owe me a favor," London said.

"It can't be anything that puts me against the queen," Algernon said.

London spit in his hand and extended it. "Done."

"Done," Algernon agreed. He did not, however, spit or reach out for a handful of London's slobber.

London laughed, far too loudly for someone who was being stealthy.

Algernon looked for a door to the Netherwhere as he walked. The entrances weren't always at the same place, but when he was summoned, one would appear. He felt the tension in his belly that meant Ebba was summoning him.

"Here!"

"The kitchen?" London scoffed. "That's where we are sneaking—"

"It's not." Algernon glanced at him before tugging open the door that had just appeared before him.

"Sacred mother of frog legs," London whispered. "That's . . . That's . . ." He shook his head and blinked. "Where did the kitchen go?"

"No idea." Algernon had very little understanding of how the doorways worked. His skin felt a sort of warm weight when the doors were near. It wasn't unpleasant, but it wasn't exactly comfortable either. The first time he'd opened one, it was simply to make that feeling stop. He knew now that the doorways appeared when he was being summoned. These temporary doors were the easy ones to enter. If he went on his own, there was another permanent gate.

"We're here," Algernon told London in a hushed voice.

They stepped forward into the Netherwhere. He heard a few more of London's muttered cusswords as he followed, but then he went silent. The first minutes in the Netherwhere weren't for speaking. The air was heavier, and it felt more like moving through water than air. Adjusting to the brighter sky was hard, too. Algernon pulled out a pair of brown-tinted goggles that he'd borrowed from his father's laboratory, as well as his backup pair. He offered these to London, who was standing at his side, wincing.

"You'll adjust," Algernon said, feeling like even his words sounded weightier here.

"We're in the Netherwhere," London whispered. "Actually. *Here.*"

"We are," Algernon agreed.

"People aren't supposed to be able to *do* this," London objected. "The Glass Castle said no one is born with the skill. They said that *once* a few of the Ravens could, and—"

"I know."

What people knew about the Netherwhere was mostly wrong. Of course. Algernon couldn't say *that* without people knowing he could go there. He didn't even tell his father. He just took a thief with him from time to time. That was it.

Neither Algernon nor London said anything further as they stared at the massive stone trees that curved and arched in a way that neither tree nor stone did in their world. Several flickers of light among the stone boughs revealed faeries zipping around in their too-fast way, and a puff of fire meant that a dragonet was nesting there. There were no humans. No giant buildings or palaces. There was no pollution. This world might be peculiar, but it was beautiful.

"Algernon!" London lurched forward, knocked over by the tentacles of some massive beast that was squishing London's face.

"Stop that," Algernon thwacked the tentacle with the sharp point he had attached to his umbrella.

"Mph. Thoungh."

"Quit trying to talk while it's on your face," Algernon told London, who was swatting at the tentacle blindly.

"I said *stop that*," Algernon repeated, poking the tentacles harder and harder. "Ebba is expecting me!"

At Ebba's name, the tentacles retracted at once and released London, who slumped to the ground.

"It hadth my thongue. My *tongue*."

The land cephalopod reached out two tentacles and awkwardly patted the boys on the heads.

"I've never seen tentacles on things that walked," London said.

"Well, you've never been to the Netherwhere . . ."

"Well, no, but—"

"Right. And you do have a point," Algernon admitted. "Tentacled beasts *should* be in the water."

"It had hold of my tongue," London stressed. "It was like a super-gross kiss or—"

"No. They think tongues are *our* tentacles," Algernon tried to explain. "It's hard for the babies to understand humans, as there aren't many of us that come here, but honestly, he was just trying to get you to talk to him."

"By yanking my tongue out?"

"I didn't say it was a good plan." Algernon shrugged, waiting to see if London would insist on going back.

But London met his gaze and asked, "Who's Ebba?"

Algernon wasn't exactly sure how to answer that. Ebba was the de facto ruler here, the keeper of wisdom, and sometimes seemed able to have every emotion at once. So all he said was, "You'll see."

The boys started walking toward the forest. There were plenty of beasts that were tucked into shadows, watching them, but he'd been granted a Writ of Crossing by Ebba, and upsetting a chimera was always a bad idea, so most of the Netherwhere creatures were friendly—of course, sometimes "friendly" meant nearly being smothered by tentacles.

"Who is Ebba?" London repeated as he chased after Algernon. He was huffing a bit from the exertion of moving in the Netherwhere.

"Ebba is a chimera."

"A what?"

"He . . . she . . . they . . . I'm not sure if Ebba is boy or girl or both." Algernon was discovering the whole boy-or-girl thing didn't matter with a lot of the Netherwhere creatures. "Ebba has the head of a lion, with a big mane of fur that fluffs out . . ."

"So, Ebba's a talking lion?"

"No . . . Ebba's back end is a serpent. That end talks too—and bites."

London frowned. "Does the lion end bite?"

"I'm not sure about biting, but it breathes fire." Algernon stepped back as a swarm of faeries flew by. They liked to try to braid things into his hair if he wasn't alert.

"Bum bites, and head burns," London said. "Great."

"And the middle sometimes has a goat head. Not always. The third head naps, and when it does, it vanishes. Awake, the goat part has horns and snapping teeth."

"Truly?"

Algernon nodded. "Yes. The tail is mean, the head is moody, and the middle is mostly rude."

"And why are we going to see a chimera?"

"THE chimera," Ebba said in a roar from all around them at once.

"Yes," Algernon agreed quickly. "THE chimera. Hello, Ebba."

"You need things?" Ebba asked, finally showing their full, immense self. Three heads—lion, goat, and serpent—all grinned. Then the goat head let out a loud yawn and vanished.

"I don't only come when I need," Algernon said to the remaining heads, politely not pointing out that Ebba had *summoned* him.

Ebba's serpent third hissed grumpily. The serpent's spit was toxic, venomous enough that it was banned in the world for everyone but the Queen's Alchemist. Algernon had a secret stash of it—even though he wasn't *technically* allowed to have it yet.

"But since I'm here, I would take some tears," Algernon said bluntly, unpacking several vials and funnels as calmly as he could while Ebba's tail end hissed and slashed through the air. At least the goat's head was resting today.

"Bring cookies next time," Ebba muttered with a rapid series of blinks. "I do like the cookies with the little red things on them."

Algernon nodded. The chimera liked meat patties—*raw* meat patties, to be precise—but Algernon had called them cookies the first time, and so they were cookies.

"I am sad when there are no cookies." Ebba sniffled, half roaring in the process. "They're beautiful, all red and dripping . . ."

"Dripping?" London echoed softly.

"The icing juice just drips from them when they squish in my teeth," Ebba explained with a wailing, whuffling noise. "It's such good cookie juice, just like a mouthful of faeries, but no wings."

"I'm not sure there will ever be cookies again," Algernon lied. "The factory where they made those is closed."

Ebba's lion head cried then. Big white tears dripped from their eyes and into the funnels that Algernon had brought for this very reason. Once the vials were full, he stoppered them and dug out a giant meat patty from his bag. He unwrapped the butcher's paper from it as Ebba watched.

"Well, I did bring *one* cookie for you," he said.

Carefully, so as not to scrape his hands on Ebba's massive teeth or raspy tongue, Algernon placed the meat patty into Ebba's lion mouth. The squelching noise made him wince. Chimeras were not tidy eaters.

Ebba nodded their furry mane and began to purr loudly when the meat was finished. From tears to purrs in a blink, Ebba cycled through emotions rapidly. Now they were staring at Algernon, looking more serious than any multiheaded purring, weeping creature should be able to do.

"You need to be careful, little human," Ebba's serpent head pronounced.

"Of?"

"Dangerous magic."

Algernon nodded. He wasn't entirely sure what Ebba meant, but Ebba spoke in mysterious ways. *Most* magic was rather dangerous.

"Come when you find what's lost," Ebba added. "I like visits from my Nightshade."

"I like my visits, too," Algernon said. "But what's the lost thing?"

"The heart," said Ebba's lion head. "The heart was lost."

"Right, then. I'll watch for a heart." Algernon nodded. He couldn't imagine finding an actual heart. That wasn't it, was it? Being the son of an alchemist, as well as an alchemist in training, meant he had seen his share of gross things, but . . . a *heart*? He shuddered.

"The heart that is found will bring hope and peace," Ebba added with a burp.

Algernon nodded again. This was the message he'd been

summoned to hear, and even though it made absolutely no sense, Algernon wrote it down to think about later.

Then he tapped London's arm and motioned toward the forest. They left, and only when they were back in Nightshade Manor did London speak. "What was *that* about?"

"A riddle of some sort. I hope." Algernon shrugged. He had no idea what Ebba meant—and he wasn't sure he wanted to know either, not if it involved finding squishy hearts.

Algernon turned to business. "One bottle of chimera tears would pay for everything we eat for a year if I had someone able to take it to Glass City to sell."

London stared at him. "And if I take it and run?"

Again, Algernon shrugged. "I am under Ebba's protection, and Ebba rules the Netherwhere beasts in our world. If I needed to find you so they could have their 'cookies,' Ebba would help me."

It was an idle threat, but London didn't need to know that. His eyes widened, but he still grinned and said, "You're as mad as your father!"

Algernon shrugged.

"Hand me the tears," London said. "I'll be happy to help."

CHAPTER 8

◆——◆——◆

Vicky

Glass City had many oddities, but one of them was the waterways where deadly things like serpents and kelpies lurked.

"Stay a little further from the canal, Vicky Love."

Her mother's words jolted Vicky. In staring at the milky surface of the water, she'd been lured closer to the canal than she'd realized. She moved away but couldn't take her eyes off a twisting wave that seemed long enough to be a serpent.

"Too small for a kelpie," she announced.

"Good." Her mother scanned the street more than the waterways.

"Do you think *she* knows we're here?" Vicky asked quietly.

The feel of her mother's protective wards snapping around them was as familiar as a hug.

"Undoubtedly. The queen always has me watched, but I will not let her control us." Vicky's mother spoke with ease now that their conversation was shielded from any ears that might overhear.

As Vicky and her mother walked further away from the city center, the crowds thinned. Few people were willing to be at the water's edge, and those who were seemed to hide their faces. Only criminals—or those who did business with them—lingered near the sea.

This was a part of the city that had been mostly abandoned when the gates of the Netherwhere had opened. The Glass Queen, not even an adult then, and her advisors had tried to negotiate with the creatures of the Netherwhere. They'd tried to order them back; they'd even tried to force them back with wards and weapons. Nothing worked. The creatures stayed, and the door stayed open.

Her mother linked arms with Vicky as they turned down a dim passageway that descended to the very edge of the sea. The canals all led here, to the area known as Steel Close, where the sea and city met. An entire herd of kelpies was kicking the water into a churning froth. They were strange-looking beasts, like massive blue horses with kelp strands for manes and fish gills in their necks.

Her mother held a sword openly now. It might be awkward to be so visibly armed within the city center, but here in the shadows of Steel Close, the flickering gas lamps illuminated blades of all sizes in most hands. There were places where weapons were simply a necessity. It made Vicky's own hand itch for a weapon.

"Now, you will need to speak firmly in the shop, Vicky," her mother instructed her. "No hesitating. If you need a minute, say that. Do not demur."

"*Never* demur," Vicky added.

"Unless it gives you the advantage." Her mother pushed open a door to a shop unlike any other Vicky had ever seen. The back wall was missing so that sea could flow into the room through the shop in a circular canal. In the center of the workshop was a firepit that glowed brightly; a few boys about Vicky's age were tending it. The hilts of several swords jutted out of both the water and the firepit.

A massive woman with arms as thick as Vicky's legs stood beside another fire, sharpening a blade.

It was all Vicky could do not to sigh in longing at the sight of all the swords on the walls and counters. Blades of various sizes, lengths, shapes, and degrees of completion were everywhere. It was breathtaking.

The woman stopped her work and shoved her goggles atop her head. "It *is* you."

"Yes, Marta, and—"

"Is she yours?" Marta nodded toward Vicky. "Or another thief?"

Vicky frowned. *A thief?* It was an odd question.

"My daughter," her mother said. "Twelfth birthday . . . and ready for a pair of swords."

"A sharp, and a blunt for practice?" Marta asked, finally stepping away from the fire.

"Yes, and a new athame," her mother added.

Marta's eyebrows lifted as she glanced at Vicky. "You work wards *and* handle blades?"

Vicky didn't reply. There were questions best not to answer. She'd been told often enough that this was one of those dangerous topics—which was why she was completely unprepared to hear her mother say, "She's my daughter in all ways."

"The others?" Marta prompted.

"Not so far. Just Vicky."

Marta looked her over. "You're just about the right age to start at Corvus now, aren't you, girl?"

Vicky stepped closer to her mother. "My parents say I can't go."

An uncomfortable quiet grew. Vicky glanced at the two children who were minding the fire. She didn't know them, and her mother hadn't raised a ward before speaking.

Marta followed her gaze and laughed. "They're ward-bound, girl; they can't tell anyone what is said or done in my shop. Plus, they know I'd feed them to the sea if they broke my trust."

Then Marta smiled so widely that the steel cap on her front tooth gleamed in the firelight. "Wouldn't be the first assistant I had to replace, now, would it?"

Vicky's mother laughed in a way that she rarely did. "Don't ever change, Marta."

The moment would've been better if Vicky hadn't seen a kelpie approaching the edge of the shop. The creature's hooves were stirring the water into whitecaps as it raced over the sea.

It was the closest she'd ever been to one. Vicky braced for its arrival, but she still covered her mouth in fright as its towering horse-shaped head poked into the shop. The sound it made was loud and piercing.

"Hush." Marta glared up at it, and it snapped its enormous teeth at her.

Both of her assistants froze.

Marta held its gaze and said, "You put out that fire again, and we're going to have words."

"Vicky?" her mother said gently. "Stay. Still."

Vicky hadn't even realized she was easing toward one of the longswords on the nearby bench. It was a new sword, no markings on the blade.

Only Vicky's years of being taught never to disobey when her mother had *that* tone saved her from snatching the sword up when the kelpie screamed. She could see her mother's hand tighten on the hilt of her own sword, but she didn't move either.

"Shoo!" Marta stomped her foot and made a large gesture, waving the kelpie off as if it were a misbehaving puppy.

The kelpie snorted out a watery breath that soaked several benches, then backed up and sank into the water as easily as rain into a puddle.

Marta walked over to a barrel and pulled out a whole raw chicken. "Good girl, Frieda." She tossed the poultry to the kelpie, who lifted up like a storm wave to catch the chicken and then left just as quickly.

The sigh of relief Vicky's mother let out made it clear that she hadn't been as calm as she had appeared. "One of these years, those things are going to eat you."

"Bah." Marta waved her hand dismissively. "One of them did take a nibble"—she hiked up her skirt and heavy leather apron to show an angry blue scar—"but I guess I'm not tasty eating."

"It bit you?" Vicky asked in awe.

Marta nodded. "It happens."

"Good thing you make swords that can cut a kelpie's hide," her mother said, reminding the swordsmith why they were there.

"Yes." Marta nodded toward a table of finished swords. "Now, let's have you pick up a few so we can get a sense of what you'll be wanting. We'll do that before we get to your athame."

Vicky did as she was told, lifting first one sword and then another. One of the assistants brought out various weapons as Marta called out numbers, letters, or codes.

"Ten crosswise," Marta finally said.

The assistant paused long enough to make Vicky notice his hesitation, but then he went to a different cupboard and pulled down a sword that was wrapped in an oily blue cloth.

The sword felt alive as Vicky brushed her hand against it. It felt like *home* when she lifted it. The weight was perfect, and the balance was even more precise than the many fine swords she'd lifted already. The hilt was wrapped in thin strips of that same cloth, but against her palm it wasn't unpleasant. It felt somehow more like an athame than a sword.

"That one's already been ordered," Marta said. "Not that *she* paid for it, but she ordered it made."

Vicky's mother clearly heard something Vicky didn't in Marta's words, because she met Marta's gaze. "I didn't think *she* was willing to lift a sword."

Marta shrugged. "It was a recent order. I didn't ask why, but she ordered it in stealth. Sent Tik to my shop. She wanted a sword no one knew of, though I'd guess you're an exception."

"I'm retired," Vicky's mother said quietly. "My only concerns are my children, and the occasional attempt at cooking a meal that's not burnt."

For a long moment, Marta said nothing. Finally, she murmured, "There are rumors of rebellion."

"Not in my home," Vicky's mother said lightly. "Would you be able to make my daughter a fitting sword?"

"I can make you one just like this. Take me a little longer than the normal sort, but . . . it might be useful to her—or you."

Her mother looked at Marta, and Vicky wasn't sure what she was missing in their conversation. All she knew was that there was a chance she could have a sword like this, and if that were so, she'd agree to whatever she must in order to make that happen.

"I'll never need another gift if I can have a sword like this," Vicky told her mother as she started to work through a sword drill—slicing through the air in strikes as if an opponent stood there.

Vicky realized she'd accidentally drawn a restoration ward with her sword, but that shouldn't have happened. Wards could only be drawn with short-bladed athames.

But then the water on the floor vanished, and the boards became unmarked. The ward had *worked*. She *had* drawn a ward with the sword!

Vicky lowered the blade so the point was aiming at the floor and looked at Marta in awe. "It's both. That's not supposed to be possible."

"There it isn't a big demand for it," Marta said blandly.

"Most ward workers are useless with a sword. And sword masters are lousy at wards. No need to make many like this."

"And I'm guessing that making such a blade is not within the skill of any other swordsmith in the Glass Empire," Vicky's mother added. "Or that such a blade is affordable."

Marta laughed. "Some people don't have to pay those rates. I'll charge you fair for the blunt sword and for the regular athame, but if this one's not going to be a Raven or—"

"She is *not*," her mother stated.

Marta gave one sharp nod before she continued, "Well, no matter what you do in life, Vicky, you're going to need a good weapon. People will notice you, so you need to have a weapon to protect you *and* draw wards to hide just how *much* you resemble your mum inside and out."

"I'm proud to be her daughter."

"And I am proud to be your mother, Vicky Love." Her mother stroked Vicky's cheek with the back of her hand, then glanced at Marta. "We shouldn't linger."

At that, Marta nodded. "Go on with you. And, Vicky, you're always welcome in my shop, girl, long as your mum says it's good by her." Marta looked far less intimidating now.

"Thank you," Vicky said. Your swords are amazing, and this is the best gift I've ever had—or hoped for."

CHAPTER 9

❖ ❖ ❖

Milan

Like many of the ragged boys in the city, Milan was practically invisible. So insignificant that most people looked away from him—which worked well for Milan, since it made them easier to rob.

Milan had learned his craft in the open air, and he continued to perfect it in the corners of the city. He remembered his earliest days in Glass City and how proud he was when he'd become adept at lifting a bit of cheese and a hunk of bread for a meal. When he'd joined Florence's house of thieves, the first thing that struck him was that the group had kettles with hot food.

Now Milan was one of the eldest and had been in Florie's house in the underground of the city for almost six years. In the beginning, Florie was just like him. Now he was in charge, and Milan was grateful for it. He'd spent half his life bedding down on a nest of blankets there, but these days, he had prime choice of which bit of floor was his own. And anything was better than the overcrowded orphanages. Milan was proud that he owned a blanket, three pairs of trousers, a coat, woolen mittens, and a pair of shoes with barely worn soles. And he had a bunch of coins stashed for a time when he'd have to move on. There wasn't much extra, but he had enough for a railway ticket to the coast and a start on passageway across the sea.

He wasn't sure what his life had been like before the street, but someone had taught him letters. He remembered that much. One of his treasures was a booklet he kept in a hidden pocket in his coat. It wasn't a proper book, at least not a whole one, but there was almost an entire chapter of a story about a boy called Jack who set off to sea. It sounded a lot better than what Milan's days were like.

Milan walked a little faster, not running, though. That was the trick: speed up and get lost in the masses but don't draw attention to yourself. Remove your cap or add a cap; maybe wrap a scarf around your throat high enough to hide your chin, too, if you can lift one from a passing stranger's neck.

Today he cut through Skinner's Close. There was to be a drop boy on the next corner. They were younger boys, not skilled enough to reach into pockets or handbags. Light fingers took practice and dexterity. Collecting a drop merely meant being able to run fast enough or fade into the streets. To survive as a thief meant working as part of a community.

"Dinner take," Milan muttered as he dropped a watch, two rings, and one money purse into Rotterdam's bin.

Rott nodded, shaking his cap loose. It was too large for his head, and there were wild curls jutting out from under it, like tiny snakes. The first goal of a thief was to get a good take, but the second was to be able to get away with it. That meant not being memorable. Milan was easy to forget: Brown hair. Brown eyes. Not too thin, too tall, too heavy, too short. He was average.

But Rott's bright corkscrew curls made him easy to remember.

"Soot or scissors for your hair tonight," Milan said.

"I don't—"

"Soot, scissors, or find a new partner." Milan folded his arms and leaned on the stone wall across from Rott. He didn't want it to look like they were friends. The police noticed that sort of thing and didn't want gangs of kids organizing.

Rott sighed. "I'll get Florie to cut it off tonight."

Milan nodded. He wasn't willing to risk everything he'd taken on a given day by having a bad partner. Technically, they were all working alone, and several thieves sometimes shared a drop person. The truth was, though, that a thief was at his best when he had a drop he could trust.

"If not, don't bother coming. I'll get someone else." Milan pushed off the wall.

"Said I'll get it cut tonight." Rott crossed his arms.

"Good," Milan said as he walked past, ready to go searching for his next target.

A short while later, he found a mother and daughter and started to follow them, studying their walk and their talk. He was surprised to see how the mother slid through the crowd. She had the graceful moves of a good thief. The girl was alert, too. She didn't move like a thief, but she saw the people here and there in the shadows. Her walk was steady, and the way she eyed him was enough to earn her a nod—and a reprieve.

There were thousands of people in the streets of Glass City—Milan would find an easier choice to relieve of their valuables. He turned away, pausing to glance upward as one of the largest gargoyles on the building dropped down low enough that the breeze from his wings caused people to stumble. For a strange moment, Milan thought that the gargoyle smiled at him.

Then the woman spotted Milan and beckoned him over. "Whose house are you?"

Milan realized the woman must have been a thief in the past. Thieves almost always recognized thieves. But thieves rarely turned into nobles—and this lady looked like a noble.

"Florie."

She nodded and pulled out a coin with his house name on it. She held the tarnished bit up and said, "Stand watch for me. No one royal and no one armed comes near without you alerting me." Then she glanced at her daughter. "Stay with him."

Her daughter stiffened. "He is to keep *me* safe?"

"Victoria," the lady said. Her tone made him think of guards, of threats, and Milan thought that he might have obeyed her without the coin.

The lady walked ahead and stopped when she met man with a long braid and a sword hanging on his side.

"Meister Tik." The lady said the man's name as if it rhymed with *meek*.

And then their words were inaudible. Whatever ward the lady had drawn blocked sound.

Milan shrugged and stood silently with the girl, watching the people pass. He would keep eyes for threats. The coin bought his diligence.

"This is absurd," Victoria said after a long, awkward pause.

Milan glanced at her.

"I am able to stand watch *and* defend myself." She glared at him.

He shrugged and continued watching every passing person.

Milan felt the draw and release of energy over and over. He glanced at her.

Her hand touched her rib cage, where he was now certain an athame hid. She continued tapping, drawing energy and releasing. It was making his head hurt.

"Can you not do that?" he asked as kindly as he could.

Victoria shot him an assessing glance. "You feel it?"

Milan gave a curt nod.

"So, you feel energy and"—she studied him—"are a . . . street criminal?"

Again, he nodded.

At that, she seemed to deflate, as if all of her temper had fled. "I shouldn't have doubted her. You're a wise choice to stand watch." She glanced at her mother. "She worries all the time about my safety."

In the process, her hand flitted in the air, drawing a hearing ward accidentally, and suddenly they heard her mother's conversation.

". . . I know *exactly* who I am, Tik! That doesn't mean the girls need to be burdened with it."

"Just be careful," the man called Tik said. "You know she

can be dangerous, Kat. She's changed so much since we were kids, and it's grown worse since you left the Ravens. Horatio seems to have her under a spell. There is talk that the war they're waging at sea is losing fighters and ships, and they need more Ravens. Horatio says—"

"Headmaster Edwards can say whatever he wants. I won't listen to that foul man."

"I will protect Vicky if you send her here. You know that," Tik said.

"Vicky will not be a Raven. She will choose her own future! I'll die before I allow the queen to make us pawns. If it's necessary to protect my family, *my cousin* will die."

"Kat!"

Milan exchanged a quick look with Victoria, who looked horrified to hear her mother so openly threaten the queen—people had gone to prison for less.

The conversation was no longer audible then. The ward the girl had accidentally drawn was erased, and it was just them again.

"I won't tell anyone what she said," he said. "Thieves' honor."

Victoria nodded stiffly at his vow. "Thank you. I owe you a favor for your silence." She held out her hand. "I am Victoria Wardrop."

Milan smothered his reaction. He'd heard of the Wardrops; everyone underground in Glass City had. He glanced again at Victoria's mother and said, "You don't owe me *anything*. It is an honor."

Then he held out the coin he'd just accepted from the

older Wardrop. "This is a thieves' coin. You can use it to get a favor—"

"So you had to help my mother when she gave it to you?" the girl interrupted.

He nodded.

From the corner of his eye, he saw her mother walking toward them and shoved the coin into Victoria's hand. "I'm Milan. That is for the House of Florence. If you ever need me or anyone of the house, use this."

Victoria dropped the coin into a pocket on her dress as her mother approached.

"We can go now," her mother said. She turned to Milan. "And my thanks to the House of Florence."

Milan felt a bit foolish. "No thanks needed, ma'am."

He watched her lead her daughter away. No other thief was as renowned as Lady Kathleen Wardrop. No other Raven was as infamous. Lady Wardrop had been the guard of the Glass Queen, the fiercest fighter and a ward mistress, and only the thieves knew she had been one of them first. Her name—like all thieves who went legit—had been changed.

I helped the legendary Lady Wardrop. Milan smiled to himself. No one would believe it. He wasn't sure he even did. He suspected that Victoria had no idea who her mother truly was or, at the least, who she had been—a thief like him. And then after becoming a Raven, she gave it all up to be a mother. He'd never had a mother, so the thought of that—of a mother who loved you enough to give everything up—was perhaps even more astounding to him than all the rest.

His own mother hadn't even wanted to keep him.

Milan shoved such thoughts away. He didn't care. Lots of people had no mother. Food wasn't free. Nothing was. And thinking about mothers wasn't going to help him fill his belly that night.

CHAPTER 10

❖————◇————❖

Milan

London?" Milan gaped at his former housemate. "You're back?"

The other thief grinned. "Not really here. Working."

"I thought you left." Milan spoke quickly, knowing that once they weren't shielded by the crush of people on the street, they wouldn't be able to keep talking.

"I did leave. I had to do a bit of business in Steel Close," London muttered.

Milan shook his head. People with any sense avoided that place. There were areas even too rough for most thieves, and that was one of them.

"You owe me," London reminded him.

Reluctantly, Milan nodded. There were a few rules that were unbreakable on the streets. You paid your debts. You kept your bargains. You never ever snitched on anyone.

"Master Nightshade is in town. When you see him, find a way to go home with him." London dug into his pockets and pulled out a bag. "Give this to the older son. You can trust him."

"Why aren't you going back?"

"I bought a ticket to a new life," London said proudly. "Boarding the ship tonight. I saved enough to start clean."

London looked over his shoulder, and then he was gone in the next moment. Not invisible. He wasn't a ward worker. He was simply skilled in the tricks of the streets. London had survived by way of skill—and luck. Some of that luck included being taken to Nightshade Manor. Being taken in there meant free food and shelter. It meant that whatever a thief earned was *all* his, not shared with the head of the house.

Whatever London had earned living there had bought him a new future.

Despite that, Milan had no desire to go to the alchemist's house, even temporarily. He liked what he did and was good at it. There were thieves in Glass City who were better, but not many. He had a light touch, and he was a good judge of character. His best plan was to get into Nightshade Manor, deliver the package, and get out.

First, he had to find the alchemist.

For the next few hours, Milan walked around the city, asking for tips from other street children, pursuing the poisoner. Finally, he saw Master Nightshade.

Tufts of hair stood out on the man's head, as if he made a habit of tugging on it when he thought. His hands were oddly stained, and unlike most men of means, there were no rings on his fingers and his hand held no ornate walking stick.

Milan picked his moment, brushed by Master Nightshade, and snagged a watch from his side pocket. It was a simple brush, distract, and lift. He folded the watch into the palm of his hand, and then he dropped it into his jacket pocket.

But true to his reputation, Master Nightshade was no easy target. He lunged forward and grabbed Milan's arm—just as Milan had planned.

Milan twisted, letting his entire body go slack at the same time, so as to use his weight to his advantage. Holding dead-weight was harder—unless you expected it. Nightshade obviously did.

"You're quick," Nightshade said approvingly.

And Milan looked up at his captor. "And you're Master Nightshade."

He released Milan's arm and asked, "Whose house?"

"Florie . . . *Florence*, sir." Milan took a step backward.

"Stop," Nightshade ordered. He studied Milan as if they weren't standing in the street, surrounded by gawking people. "You clearly have all your limbs and both eyes. Good. How are your teeth?"

"My teeth?"

"I see some, but"—he grabbed Milan's cheeks and squeezed until his mouth opened—"are they all in there? And any sores?"

"In my mouth?" Milan stumbled slightly as Nightshade released him.

"On your skin, boy. I have a powder for any vermin on you, but—"

"I don't have bugs *or* sores," Milan snapped. He added the

word *now* silently in his head. There was a thing with lice a few months ago, but that had passed.

"Well, come on, then," the alchemist said. "I have things to do."

Milan hesitated. He *knew* what was happening. He'd planned for it. But he still hesitated. Nightshade was the man who mixed death and pain for their queen.

But a debt was a debt, and Milan owed London.

So he followed the alchemist to a carriage and boarded it for the long trip to Nightshade Manor. Whatever he was carrying to the eldest Nightshade son was obviously important if London had used up his debt to get it to him. Milan tried to ignore his fears as the carriage rattled further and further away from the familiar comforts of the streets of Glass City.

The foliage was brighter out here, and the plants had blossoms as bright as noblemen's clothes. The cloak of smog that was inescapable in Glass City was absent. Seeing such a world made Milan realize perhaps he had missed a lot by living in the city.

Finally, they turned into a long drive that led up to an ominous-looking house, and the carriage came to a halt beside an algae-filled fountain.

"Climb down, Milo," Master Nightshade instructed him.

"Milan," the thief corrected as he clambered to the ground and took in the manor house. It was a vast gray stone thing, with towers jutting out in odd directions. One, in particular, stuck out from the edge of a room as if a storm had blown it in and deposited it where the wind had stopped.

As he was staring at the house, a tall boy who looked to be

about Milan's age came out of the massive front door. His steps faltered briefly as he saw Milan standing there, but he continued forward.

"Algernon," Master Nightshade said. "I think we have at least one more mask left." He rummaged in a pocket and, after a moment, pulled out a scrap of paper on which he had a tally of masks. He read it triumphantly. "Two, even!"

"Yes, Father."

"Well, I only brought one houseguest." He pointed at Milan. "Milfred here—"

"Milan," Milan interrupted.

"Milly will need a cot, and he ought to have a visit to the debugging tub," Master Nightshade continued.

"I don't have any bugs."

"And clothes to wear while these are laundered." The man squinted at Milan. "I think he's been fed well enough, though, so he can work tonight."

The boy, Algernon, nodded and walked away.

After a moment, Master Nightshade noted, "Algernon is my son. My *heir*."

That was the boy Milan needed to see, but there was no graceful way to call him back and give him the package from London, and Milan was fairly sure that he shouldn't tell Master Nightshade about it.

"The fountain is dangerous," the alchemist said as he started toward the house. "Water serpents in there. Some very fine knitting algae, too . . . but you mustn't reach into the water unless you have the gloves."

Milan trudged behind the alchemist, finding it difficult to

keep pace after he'd been rattled around atop the carriage. He was already feeling tender in spots.

"Gloves?" he prompted.

"Thick boar hide. The serpent's fangs can't get through them."

Milan nodded again.

"And Milton?" the poisoner said.

"Yes?" Milan was not going to correct him again.

"Check for any fangs that break off on the gloves. Useful thing, serpents' teeth. Not quite the same as chicken's teeth, but still very important."

"Right," Milan agreed. "Check for teeth if I reach into the water where the poisonous serpents live."

The alchemist strode into the house then, and Milan followed. He'd come this far. He wasn't going to turn back now. He'd give the Nightshade boy the package and get out of this strange house.

CHAPTER 11

◆———◆———◆

Rupert

Rupert watched the thief stalk the older Nightshade. It made him smile. Well, as much a gargoyle smiled. The effort of turning a stone face into a human expression was slow, and he often found himself distracted midway.

Kat used to stalk Nightshade much the same way. She also had stalked Tik, but he caught her quickly.

Not Nightshade . . .

She dropped from a ledge, not quite knocking the boy to the ground.

"Kat!" Nightshade fumbled his book and tried to pull out a small version of the swords Tik and Kat were always waving in the air.

"Slow," she said. "What will become of you when I'm dead?"

"You can't die."

Kat sighed. "I'll be her guard. I'll die before any of you. Best start making friends with other thieves, dear."

Nightshade sputtered at her, and she hugged him. Rupert smiled at the memory.

Like the others, Rupert had loved her best—and always tried to protect her.

Feathers fell and hit her pursuers.

Talons tore into soft creatures.

Tik started to notice.

Then others noticed.

And when the queen noticed, she was not happy. All of a sudden, she disliked the gargoyles who dared to give their allegiance to someone else. Around that time, she *changed*. She was suddenly more like her advisors. Colder. More serious. There was no more laughter. No real smiles from the queen—not even for Tik.

Nightshade knew something had changed. Rupert suspected things. Tik wept in private.

Kat left. She started a new life, one without palaces or visits in private with the queen. She took Wilbur, and they left the court for good and started a family.

Through all of it, Rupert stayed near Kat. He looked after Tik, Nightshade, and Sweeney, too, but Kat was special. She was his purpose. His mission.

And then there were little ones. Nightshade and Kat both had sprogs of their own. Rupert and his kind watched over them.

Nightshade collected children, too. This newest one, Milan, was one of them, and Rupert admired the way he moved. Milan would befriend the alchemist's boy, and Rupert saw it and was glad. One more for him to guard and guide.

Rupert would do whatever he could to protect them all.

He'd help them see that each choice in life mattered. Each small moment of courage and each time love overcame fear added up.

With enough small ripples, entire oceans could be shifted. These acts—of love, of loyalty, of justice—would one day build into a mighty force that would create a great change.

That was why Rupert stayed here: to help them see how powerful their ripples were, even though they couldn't see it yet. Like the now-adult children, these ones were his mission. His purpose.

CHAPTER 12

◆———◆———◆

Vicky

When Vicky returned home, she thought a lot about Corvus, about swords and wards and learning from teachers other than her parents. She didn't want to leave her family, but sometimes she imagined what it would be like to go to a school. She dreamed of meeting other kids, of learning, of adventures.

Although Vicky wasn't sure *what* she wanted to do when she grew up, she knew that being a spy or a soldier or an alchemist wasn't it. Sometimes she wished there were a job that was just reading. That sounded like the best job. Swords for fun, books for work—Vicky could do *that* job.

"Vicky, where are you?"

"Here," she called. Vicky was nestled into the corner of her favorite sofa. The light here was perfect, and the spot where she was had that warm coziness that made it as comfortable as a bed but also easier to sit upright to see the pages of her book.

"You need to get ready," her mother said.

Vicky closed her book, keeping her thumb in the place

where she'd paused. It really was a lovely story, one in which a girl fell into another world and had a grand adventure.

"Up with you," her mother said in that tone parents get when they are pretending to be cheerful. "You cannot go before the queen in nightclothes."

"The queen?"

"Tonight," her mother said. "The queen *demands* that we come tonight. The messenger just came."

Her mother took Vicky's hand and squeezed. "And I shall accompany you. I'll be with you the whole time, whether *she* likes it or not."

"I want to meet her," Vicky said carefully. "I'm not afraid."

"You should be. We all should be."

"Some people like her. Maybe she's changed since you—"

"She has not." Her mother put on a fake smile. "Now, come. I have a dress for you."

As Vicky followed her mother out of the library, she was surprised when her mother turned and pulled her close. The hug wasn't shocking, but the suddenness of this one was. Sometimes when their mother acted like this, their father would pull the girls aside—or occasionally just Vicky—and explain that there had been an Incident elsewhere.

Incidents were frightening, even for someone like Kathleen Wardrop, who was better with swords and daggers than most of the queen's generals. On the days immediately after an Incident, the girls all had to stay with either her or their father almost nonstop. More than once, Vicky had woken to the sound of her mother checking the windows and laying new wards.

"If I should be afraid, why are we going?"

"Because *she* is the queen, and on this, we must obey." Her mother was already walking away. "Lizzie will help you with your dress. Your father will simply have to help me dress *and* chase Alice."

In books, wealthy families had nannies or governesses to look after the wee ones and teach them their lessons. Parents were the sorts of creatures who drifted into the nursery like friendly ghosts to dust their children's cherubic cheeks with kisses. Kathleen and Wilbur Wardrop were very much *not* like book parents. They were the children's everything: cook and cleaner, teacher and lecturer.

The closest the kids had come to a caretaker was when they were left alone with the house gargoyles for security. But gargoyles didn't read stories or help with sums.

"I have your dress," Lizzie said from behind her. "Mother gave it to me to bring over. And a spare athame."

Lizzie held out the smallish knife.

As Vicky took it, she met one of the house gargoyles' eyes. He was a favorite of hers. She had called him Uncle Millicent years ago when she first spoke to him, and he'd seemed to like being called uncle.

"Be cautious, niece." He shifted his feet on the ledge outside her window and craned his neck toward her. When he stretched it out, it was as long as an uncoiling serpent.

"I'll be in the Glass Castle. There's nowhere safer," she thought-spoke to him.

"Not even the *queen* is safe there anymore."

Vicky met Uncle Millicent's gaze again. "I'll be careful. I promise."

The old gargoyle smiled at her.

Lizzie tapped her shoulder. "Vicky? Stop daydreaming. You need to dress."

"What color is my dress?" Vicky asked. She didn't care as much about dresses as she did about wards or books or swords, but she knew Lizzie did.

"It's a dark-green one I'd never even *seen*. Mother had it in her closet from when she wore court dresses," Lizzie said. "It's so beautiful."

Lizzie helped her into the things she needed to wear to meet the queen. The chemise was easy, but Lizzie then had to lace the corset. It was the same one Vicky had worn on her birthday.

Vicky held the athame against her skin, feeling its energy flow into her. She braced for the corset tightening, but it didn't come.

"Lizzie?"

"Mother said to leave it looser in case you needed air," she said softly.

She thought of reasons she might need extra air: gasping in fear or effort. She didn't think she'd be *that* afraid of meeting the queen, or that she'd be fighting or running. Those were the only logical reasons to need to breathe deeper, but between gargoyle warnings and loose corsets, she was growing fearful.

"Loose is good," Vicky said.

After she was properly dressed, boots on her feet and gloves on her hands, she hugged Lizzie and kissed Alice. Then she took an umbrella from the stand at the door and went toward the carriage.

Poppa stood beside Vicky's mother, holding an umbrella over her head. He wasn't bothering with one. He'd be staying home with her sisters, so getting a little wet didn't matter. Her mother, on the other hand, was dressed in a fine deep-red dress with a black cape and hat. She looked a bit frightening, as if she were dressed for a battle.

Vicky didn't need to ask if she wore weapons under her skirt. The way she stood was different when she was fully armed. Her spine was straighter, and her motions were closer to those of a dancer.

Her father kissed Vicky's cheek. Then he helped her and her mother into the carriage. It was grander than the one they usually used, but Vicky supposed that going to Glass Castle required their finest option. Her family didn't like things that demonstrated wealth or drew attention. Tonight, though, the rules were different. No one could go to the castle without showing their best face.

"Be safe," he told them as he closed the door. Then he called out to the driver—who sat outside the enclosed box—to start.

As Vicky settled into the carriage, she felt a flush of excitement. The queen, the actual *queen*, had asked to meet her. That was a sort of adventure. Not going away to school without her family, but still, it was new. And new was rare enough that a bubble of excitement filled Vicky's belly. But worry crept in, too.

"Why me?" Vicky asked.

"Well, Vicky Love, because you can already work wards better than most adults. There've only been two other girls like that."

"I know one was you," Vicky said, "but who was the other?"

After a pause, her mother whispered, "The queen."

"Really?"

"It's quite rare. Only a few people can do what you do so young," she said. "*And* use blades as if they were magic. People used to say that meant we were destined to be warriors, heroes of the people, to be born with so much talent. It makes people think you will do great things."

"Like you."

Mama laughed.

Vicky reached over and squeezed her mother's hand. "You're the bravest, strongest, best person I know."

Her mother nodded and turned to watch the rain outside the carriage. "I was a fine Raven. I could walk in there tonight, and there are very few people who could stop me. *She* knows that. It's why she keeps us under watch."

"But you protected the queen."

"Yes. But she grew afraid of me. A lot of them did." She smiled at Vicky. "Your old mother was a very scary fighter, and a weapon without a master is dangerous to the throne. I gave my word not to oppose her, Vicky. In exchange, she set me free."

"Are you changing your mind?" Vicky asked.

"Only if she threatens you. Or your sisters." Kathleen Wardrop sounded more like a mother dragon than a lady. "Then I'd burn down everything she holds dear to keep you safe."

The rest of the trip was spent in silence. The only sounds were of wheels turning, carriage creaking, and rain falling.

It would have been enough to lull Vicky to sleep if not for the fear mixed in with the excitement of going to court.

"Everything is going to be fine," Vicky said, wishing there were a ward she could draw to make words true.

"Of course it is," Mama said with a squeeze of her hand. "For as long as I draw breath, I'll never let anything happen to you, Vicky Love."

CHAPTER 13

◆——◇——◆

Vicky

Vicky thought the exterior of the Glass Castle was everything a castle should be. Sharp, beautiful spires jabbed into the sky. And lights made the castle seem to glimmer in the dark like a beacon.

Inside the gates, guards waited, watching them as they crossed. A hush descended, as if seeing Kathleen Wardrop was enough to terrify their tongues so much that speaking was impossible.

They nodded to Vicky, bowed to her mother, and did nothing to aid or stop the two from entering the great foyer. The floor of the entry hall was a mosaic of shattered glass, and branching out from it there were at least nine different hallways.

"Come," her mother said. She led her down a hall decorated in clear glass with spots of red and violet. Vicky followed her to the end, and they arrived in the throne room.

At the center of the room was Queen Evangeline on her throne, with a row of Ravens standing behind her. She was dressed in a shimmering red-and-gold dress, and tiny jewels decorated her hair. Queen Evangeline was both beautiful and frightening, and Vicky stumbled.

Her mother steadied her. "I'm right here, Vicky Love."

As they walked toward the queen, Vicky noticed people chatting in small groups while musicians played and faeries spun around the chandeliers. Having faeries inside was dangerous, but perhaps even they obeyed the Glass Queen.

"She favors you," the queen said as Vicky and her mother stopped in front of the throne. "Seeing her is like seeing you all those years ago."

"She is my daughter. Of course she *looks* like me. All of my girls do."

"And do you work wards like your mother?" the queen asked.

Vicky glanced at her mother, who nodded slightly.

"I do," Vicky admitted.

"Show me," the queen ordered. She leaned forward a little, and Vicky almost asked how she could bend while wearing a corset. Perhaps queens had special corsets? Perhaps they didn't have to wear them? The temptation to ask faded quickly when she saw how tense her mother had become.

Vicky debated whether to reach for the athame under her dress or use the one under her corset, but her mother's hand dropped onto her shoulder.

"I'm giving her my athame," Mama said. Her tone was the super-calm one that meant she was Not Calm. All the eyes in the room were on them as her mother released the athame on her wrist. It meant Vicky could hide how many athames she had on her.

Vicky took the small knife in her hand and sketched a quick rune for silence. As soon as she did so, she realized that she'd been so nervous that she'd cast a strong enough ward that it locked out the queen herself . . . in front of her throne . . . with witnesses. Vicky glanced at the queen worriedly, but she didn't look angry.

Instead, Queen Evangeline was smiling.

The only sound Vicky could hear was breathing. It always sounded louder in the complete silence of privacy wards.

Mama looked down, hiding her face so no one could read her lips as she spoke. "Lower it slowly, Vicky Love. You are letting fear make you forgetful. Keep it simple. We've practiced this. Appear unremarkable."

Vicky took extra time to draw the next rune. It wasn't hard to lower her own ward, but she made herself go slowly and tried to falter a little. Revealing how naturally ward work came to her would be dangerous. She knew that. Mama had told her so for her whole life.

"How extraordinary," the queen said. Her eyes looked a bit like the glossy sheen of beetles, hard and slick. It made Vicky want to take a step backward.

"She's already twelve," Mama said. "It's a simple ward."

"I know how old your children are, Kathleen." The queen didn't look away from Vicky as she spoke. "Can you do offensive wards? Cut with air? Sever? Remove water from forms?"

"No," Vicky and her mother both said at the same time.

"None at all?"

"I *could* technically, but I will not. Mama disapproves of

80

violence," Vicky explained. "I know protection wards, a few wards for gates . . . useful ones."

The queen glanced at Mama. "Offensive wards aren't useful?"

"No. To strike first, to invite offense, is a corruption of wards. The best *offense* with wards is to use them defensively—as they were intended," Mama said. "I learned that from *you*, Your Majesty."

The queen tensed, and the Ravens behind her drew their blades.

"You know I could reach you first," Mama said in a very quiet voice. "Unlike my daughter, I am adept at offensive wards."

The queen raised her hand, and Vicky saw that it was trembling. The Ravens all stopped moving. Everything felt too tense, and Vicky wanted it to be calmer.

"I'm better at weapons than wards," Vicky blurted out, trying to find a way to keep things from becoming even more uncomfortable.

The queen glanced at her.

"Your Majesty," Vicky added belatedly.

The queen smiled then.

"And are swords not *offensive*?" she asked in that tone adults use when they think they think they know the answer they'll get.

"Many of the same cuts that are used for attack are used in defense, so you can't know one without the other, Your Majesty. Just like with defensive wards."

The queen studied her, and Mama stayed perfectly still.

The energy to draw wards any moment was so high that Vicky felt sick in the stomach. Maybe the rest of the people standing in the queen's throne room didn't feel it. Vicky glanced around at them. Only one person seemed to be staring at Mama with the same queasy expression that Vicky felt—a girl in a bright-blue dress.

Vicky sent a little pulse toward the girl. No more than a finger reaching out to her, but the girl in blue felt the poke. Her attention switched to Vicky, and not gently. Before the sparks of being investigated grew uncomfortable, Vicky shoved a wall of energy toward her, but it was too forceful. The girl stepped back and stumbled.

"Vicky Love?" Mama asked.

"I'm fine."

"Meredith?" the queen called.

The girl recovered her footing. She was lovely, elegant in every way, with wide blue eyes, a heavy fringe of dark lashes, and a slightly upturned nose. Her voice was as musical as such an image demanded as she replied, "I'm sorry, Queen Evangeline. My mistake."

"You *are* very like your mother, aren't you?" the queen said happily to Vicky. "You'd do well here."

Mama bowed her head. "I am but a discarded knife. No longer sharpened or drawn."

The queen made a noise that might have been a laugh and said, "You know you are still difficult . . . to replace."

Briefly, Mama lifted her gaze; she drew a silencing ward between one blink and the next; no one outside their conversation could hear her. "My daughters. My freedom. In exchange, you had my blade at your side, and you still have my silence."

"I remember the terms, *cousin*," the queen pronounced. "Send the girl to Corvus at least."

"To Horatio Edwards? No."

"Let her learn. Train. And then *she* can decide for herself someday. I'm not a fool, Kat. She's as gifted as you are. And these are gifts intended to protect the empire. It's her *duty*, just like it was yours and mine. Think about that."

The queen stood, and everyone else—including Vicky—kneeled, curtsied, or bowed.

The queen waited until they were all showing their respect, and then she said, "Rise. Enjoy the evening." She stepped down from her dais, directly in front of Vicky.

"If you ever change your mind, Victoria, there will be a place for you. I am here if ever you need me. You will *always* be welcome."

CHAPTER 14

◇————◇————◇

Milan

Milan woke with a startle. He was in a room full of boys at the Nightshade house. The windows were immense, and moonlight poured in on the thieves as they rested in their cots. Baskets or luggage beside each cot functioned as a wardrobe of sorts, giving each resident of the enormous room some space of his own.

The nursery spanned half an entire floor of the manor. There were four doors, too, so several exits were available. Exits mattered enough to Milan that he'd taken the cot halfway between two doors. Sometimes proximity to a single door was a disadvantage. If that door was barricaded, you were trapped. By being between two exits, Milan had choices.

As one of the doors opened, he felt like he'd made a wise choice.

Milan was relieved to see Algernon step into the room. Earlier that evening, Milan had slipped a note to him saying, "London sent me."

He watched as Algernon looked around the nursery. His

gaze tracked over the sleeping thieves, the assorted boots and shoes under the edges of beds, and eventually to the crack in the window at the very end of the room. He frowned at that.

"Come on," Algernon said in a quietish voice.

Milan stood and shoved his feet into his boots. He was still dressed, although he'd noticed that a lot of the thieves seemed comfortable enough to sleep in nightshirts. A few had teased that the "new ones" always were like him. Milan had shaken their words off.

He wasn't generally concerned by people's words, especially since they were usually spoken to manipulate him. Part of life among thieves was learning to ignore the barbs. Maybe it was that the other thieves were trying to toughen you up for your own good. Maybe it was simply their sense of humor. Either way, slings and barbs were inevitable.

Now, when they stepped into the hallway, Milan handed Algernon the package. "From London."

Algernon shook his head in what looked like disappointment. "He's not coming back, then."

"No."

"Are you staying?" Algernon asked.

Milan hadn't known what to expect Algernon Nightshade to be like, but he certainly hadn't expected him to be standing outside a room full of sleeping thieves, looking sad that one of them wasn't returning to this strange manor house.

Algernon motioned for Milan to go further along the hallway as he spoke. "London is gone. I need someone to come with me on an errand, and he sent you."

"I just came to deliver a package," Milan pointed out. Despite himself, he asked, "What was in it?"

"Money." Algernon shrugged. "Now . . . I need to go to the Netherwhere. Will you come?"

"Did you just say what I think you said?"

"I did." Algernon sighed. "Just come with me. London trusted you, or he wouldn't have sent you."

He started to walk away.

Milan had two choices: try to sleep, or follow Algernon.

Curiosity won. The boys descended to the main floor of the house, and Algernon ushered Milan inside a room and then swung a heavy metal bar down so the door couldn't be opened from the outside.

"No one here knows I can find my way into the Netherwhere," Algernon said. "Likely, nothing bad will happen tonight, but I can't promise that."

Milan snorted. "Do you really expect me to believe you can go to another world?"

Algernon just shrugged and got to work grabbing some gloves and a couple of satchels from a shelf. Then he lifted the edge of the rug. Under it was a trapdoor.

"Grab on," Algernon ordered.

"If I go with you, wherever it is, I expect payment," Milan told him.

"One coin," Algernon offered.

"Six."

Algernon dug into a bag, pulled out three coins, and held them out. "Deal?"

"Deal," Milan repeated, accepting the three coins with an open palm.

"Pull," Algernon ordered, with a nod to the trapdoor.

Both boys took hold of an oversized ring, tarnished to the point of looking more like steel than brass. They heaved until the floor lifted, revealing a dark tunnel.

Now, Milan had crept through his share of unpleasant places. He'd even taken shortcuts through the nasty sewage tunnels one morning. It had been that or get taken in by the police. But tonight? Was he really going to drop into this dark pit? Was it a trap? People weren't really able to go to the Netherwhere, were they?

"Wherever this leads, I can watch out for myself," Milan said.

"Good." Algernon dropped to his belly, reached an arm into the darkness, and pulled a lantern out of the hole. He tinkered with it, twisting a valve and rolling up a wick. Then he lit the thing and announced, "Let's go."

Milan nodded. If Algernon was game for creeping through a dark tunnel, Milan was going, too.

CHAPTER 15

Algernon

A lgernon tried to seem more relaxed than he felt. The journey to the Netherwhere when he wasn't being summoned could be difficult, so he was glad to have company. At least when he was summoned by Ebba, the trip was quicker—and he knew someone would be on the lookout for his arrival.

"First or second?" he prompted when Milan still hadn't moved.

"What?"

"Do you want to go first or second?"

Without replying, Milan took a deep breath and started down the ladder.

Algernon waited until Milan was on the third rung before lowering the lantern further. It cast enough light that the passage was dancing with shadows. Small things skittered away into the darkness, but that was simply the way of tunnel travel. There were worse things waiting on the other side, ones not likely to run from light. Those were the scary ones.

"Here." Algernon lowered the lantern as far as he could, so Milan could take it. Climbing one-handed was foolish. It was another reason to take someone into the Netherwhere with him.

Milan reached up and took the lantern, and Algernon shinnied down the ladder.

"You're quick for a rich kid," Milan said.

Algernon grinned. "And you're smart for a thief."

"You really think we're going to the Netherwhere, don't you?"

"We are. I need faery wings." Algernon saw no harm in admitting what he was after. "It's easiest to get the wings this way."

Milan looked suspicious. "You want me to go somewhere and pull wings off faeries?"

"No!"

"Alchemists are often a little bonkers," Milan said gently. "Maybe we ought to go back—"

"In the Netherwhere," Algernon said loudly, "the faeries shed their wings. Over here, they aren't able to shed—so collecting them in our world *hurts* the faeries."

Algernon couldn't bring himself to do that.

"They bite," Milan grumbled. "I'm not getting a faery bite for three coins."

Algernon rolled his eyes. "I might ask them to bite you if you keep complaining."

"It's usually the *old* alchemists who've sniffed too many fumes."

Algernon ignored him. He'd see soon enough. The thieves always doubted at first.

When they reached the gates at the end of the tunnel, Algernon turned to Milan and said, "Just don't say anything to anyone. Watch your step. Watch your hands. I have permission to be there, so just stay with me."

Milan's expression was still skeptical. "Sure. I'll stick to you in 'the Netherwhere.'"

"Here we go." Algernon thrust a finger into the oversized keyhole in the gate. He felt a tiny hand holding his finger steady—and then a bite.

A cold forked tongue tickled the bite. That was the only reason Algernon had to believe that the owner of the teeth wasn't a faery. Faeries didn't have split tongues.

"Put a finger in and hold it still." Algernon pointed at the giant keyhole that he'd just removed his own finger from.

Milan glanced at the blood on Algernon's finger, but he still shoved his finger in to be bitten. He barely flinched. He did, however, scowl at Algernon.

The gate seemed be drawing in a great breath. It wasn't, as far as Algernon could guess. He'd studied it often enough, but he was no closer to figuring it out than he had been the first time he'd opened it. There was something between science and magic that caused the things tied to the Netherwhere to act as they did. It was a land that obeyed its own sense of logic, not quite science or only magic. It was neither. Once, it had been called the Neitherwhere, before it was shortened to the Netherwhere.

Algernon pulled out goggles and two hats from his bag and handed a set to the thief. He slipped on his goggles and tugged a hat down over his head until all of his hair was covered.

They stepped forward into the Netherwhere, and Milan looked at him, wide-eyed.

"Hurry" was all Algernon said, trying not to waste breath as his body adjusted to the thicker air in the Netherwhere.

The hum of wings exploded as faeries surged forward like a cloud of insects, intent on ripping hair out in fistfuls. Algernon wasn't sure why they wanted it or what it was for, but he wasn't in the habit of giving anything away for free.

Milan was gripping the sides of his hat, trying to protect his head. "Back," he huffed at them. "Back, you winged monsters!"

Algernon snatched a faery from the air. "He is my *guest*."

The faery in his hand stopped moving. Its wings went slack, and if not for his grip on the creature, it would have plummeted to the ground.

Then, all at once, every faery stopped moving. It was as if they shared a hive mind. Algernon had thought on more than one occasion that they might.

One of the gargoyles craned its serpentine neck their direction, watching them in the studious way of gargoyles.

Then one faery darted away from the swarm and returned in quick order, toting a sewn-leaf sack that bulged with its contents.

Once the faery was in reach, Algernon held out a hand, and the little creature dropped the sack into his outstretched palm. Then Algernon took out the tiny bag he had brought as payment. He paid them with bits of sheep's wool and assorted beetle shells.

The faeries fluttered their sharp-edged wings in unison and then departed as abruptly as they had arrived.

At his side, Milan asked quietly, "Can I speak yet?"

Algernon shrugged.

"We're in the Netherwhere," Milan said with a bit of awe. "But you're still bonkers."

Algernon grinned. He liked that thieves understood him, that they realized he wasn't just the boy who would be spending his life in a lab. "Maybe."

"So, this is it. A new world, but as mad and beautiful as ours," Milan said, looking around at the bright, strange place that was home to many of the creatures that lived in the world he knew. "Why don't any humans live here?"

"No clue." Algernon shrugged.

Milan stared at the bit of the Netherwhere around them. "It would be . . ."

"Wonderful," Algernon finished. He'd fantasized about it but knew it was wishful thinking. "But right now, we need to pick up a few more things that aren't offered so freely."

Milan smiled a thief's smile and said, "Excellent. I'm good at picking up things."

Algernon's smile split his face. It was good to have a friend, no matter which world he was in.

◇ ◇ ◇

CHAPTER 16

Milan

Milan hadn't expected either of Master Nightshade's sons to accept him, but after the trip to the Netherwhere, he and Algernon had developed a bond. It wasn't friendship exactly, but for now it was close enough to it that Milan felt like staying at Nightshade Manor for a bit longer.

They couldn't be *real* friends, of course. Algernon was manor-born, and Milan was . . . Actually, he had no idea where he came from. There were times he had vague memories of parents. He knew that someone had taught him letters, plants, geography, sums, and assorted other skills that most of the ragged boys lacked. That had to mean somebody had cared for him once.

They were good memories, but Milan had learned it was usually best to keep his skills secret. Thieves weren't meant to know most of what he did. Knowledge was for the high class, not the street-raised.

Today, however, he made a mistake.

"What's the second step?" Master Nightshade had just said

to himself. They were in the dim lab, and he was frustrated that he couldn't read the steps from across the room.

"Dice the tubers." Milan had read the instructions aloud without thinking. He'd looked right at the instructions and *read them*.

The silence that followed was as thick as the smoke that lingered in the lab most weeks. Milan felt wretched; his secret ability to read had been exposed by his own foolishness.

"You read . . . And what else can you do, Milly?" the alchemist said.

Milan shrugged. "Bit of this. Some of that. Nothing that would make me trouble to you . . . sir."

Nightshade blinked at him in that odd way of his, where it seemed like he was trying to clear away something in his eyes.

Milan backed up. He didn't reach for the glass beakers on the table or the vials with the powdered poisons, but he scanned the room, noting various weapons.

"Do you read all of my formulas?"

"Why would I do that?" Milan stared directly at him as he deflected the question. "I'm not a proper apprentice. Got no need to read your cookbooks."

"But you could."

Now Milan wrapped his fingers around a vial of poison that would knock a person out.

Nightshade looked at his choice and rewarded him with a rare smile. "You're clever, aren't you?"

Milan shrugged.

"Well, it's a waste to kill you after you went to the trouble

94

of stalking me to get invited to my house," the alchemist said, almost as if he were talking to himself.

"When I what?"

"Stalked me," the master alchemist said. "Not very gracefully either. You can't think a man like me hasn't been stalked before, can you?"

He broke into a wheezy laugh.

"I can go," Milan said. He backed toward the staircase.

Nightshade snorted. "With my formulas in your head? No, I'd rather keep you here. You have a knack for the work, anyhow," Master Nightshade said. "But why did you stalk me?"

"London had a package for your boy," Milan admitted.

"Ah. Smart boys, my sons." Nightshade nodded. "I wondered where they'd found the extra money."

The alchemist didn't ask anything else. He tugged at his tufts of hair as he looked at the piles of herbs and plants on the counter, waiting to be prepped. Finally, he said, "You have use to me, so don't run."

Milan stood there staring, his hand still wrapped around a vial of poison, as the alchemist started dicing the tubers. Could he run? Did he want to? He weighed the idea of being Master Nightshade's apprentice. There were paths that opened up for the boys who ended up at Nightshade Manor. Of course, some of them also died, or came back with such coughs and pains that they might as well be dead.

"You'll need supplies," the alchemist said.

"Sir?"

"I don't imagine you have suitable clothes or even a trunk," he continued.

"A trunk?"

"Read the next step."

Milan glanced at the recipe. "Foxglove."

"Get the black gloves for both of us . . . What do they call you?"

"Milan."

The alchemist lifted his gaze and sized him up again. "Right, then. *Milan*. There's an old trunk in the attic. You'll need to make sure it's serviceable. Look around up there for any clothes that fit, too."

Milan handed Nightshade a pair of gloves and slipped a pair onto his hands.

"Why do I need a trunk?" Milan asked.

"For school, boy. Can't be arriving at the school with your things all wrapped in a cord like so much rubbish." Master Nightshade grabbed a stalk of foxglove and started steaming it. His attention was now on the wilting plant, so he'd obviously missed seeing Milan's open mouth.

"You'll come with us and learn to be one of the Queen's Ravens," the Master continued. "It's either that, or I send you off to one of the workhouses."

School. That was a thing too precious to even dream about, an award so far out of reach for a ragged boy that Milan had never even fantasized about it.

"School," Milan whispered.

"Or the workhouse." This time there was an almost-joking tone to the alchemist's voice.

"School," Milan repeated again as he stepped closer to the most skilled poisoner in the empire. He didn't know how or why the man was sending him to school instead of punishing him for his ability to read. It didn't matter. Nothing else mattered now. Milan was going to learn. He was going to be elevated beyond the alleys, beyond even the cherished but damp corner of Nightshade Manor he now called his.

He glanced at the alchemist again. "I'm going to school."

"So it seems. So it seems."

Milan went from being excited to remembering that nothing in this world was ever so easy. He stared at the alchemist and asked, "Why?"

"You'll be useful to me, to my son, to the queen," Master Nightshade said. "Clever hands and loyalty are useful skills for a Raven."

"I'll find the trunk," Milan said.

"Indeed," Master Nightshade said. "Wise choice, Milo. Wise choice."

And Milan shook his head. Whatever madness the alchemist had, Milan was starting to think a fair bit of it was an act. The man smiled at him as if they were both in on a secret—but Milan wasn't quite sure what the secret was.

CHAPTER 17

◆ ◇ ◆

Vicky

The days after the trip to Glass City were tense. A message had arrived from the queen, inviting Vicky to attend Corvus School.

"She *cannot* do that!" Kathleen said.

Vicky's father, Wilbur, said, "She can, Kat. She's the *queen*. We can do nothing but try to resist . . . or give in."

"Vicky is *my* daughter."

"And mine," her father added quietly.

Vicky's mother stood at the kitchen window and said, "Maybe we were wrong to stay here. We could leave the country."

"Where would we go? This is our home. There's nowhere safer," her father said. "The wards here are nearly impenetrable."

"Nearly," her mother echoed. "Is 'nearly' good enough?"

Vicky crept into the kitchen and asked, "Would it be better if I agree to go to Corvus?"

Her parents exchanged a look before her father answered. "The school isn't a bad place. We were both happy there, but things have changed. Headmaster Horatio Edwards wants more power—and he doesn't care who he injures along the way. He's always been corrupt, but it's gotten worse in the last few years."

"Yes, there is that," her mother said. "But it's what comes *after* the school that worries me. Serving the palace is dangerous. You should be able to *choose* to be a Raven or not. Choices are important, Vicky Love. Small or big ones. They all add up. I didn't have any when I was your age."

"Why does the queen want *me*?" Vicky asked softly. "Are you *actually* cousins? What's going on?"

Her father sighed. "Let's all sit down."

Once the three of them were gathered around the table, he began. "A very long time ago, the queen cared for your mother."

Her mother snorted rudely.

"She did care, Kat," he said. Then he looked at Vicky and continued. "But the queen changed. She gave up her ideals. And she hated it when your mother chose to leave her service—and took me with her."

He glanced at his wife. "I wasn't as good as your mother, but *no* Ravens had ever left. We lived, served, and died for the Glass Queen."

"But if the queen didn't want you to leave her, why did she let you?" Vicky asked.

"Probably because it was best for both of us. We were both

strong and stubborn," her mother said, "but I guess I was stronger than the queen, and she had to let me go."

LATER THAT NIGHT, Vicky discovered that she was sleep-walking again when she woke to find herself in the window seat.

She wasn't sure what had woken her, so she walked through the house, feeling the wards. Her mother's wards were some of the best that could be, so there was no reason for worry. Something had roused her, though.

"Vicky?" Her mother's voice came from the dark. "Did you hear something?"

"Felt it," Vicky said, realizing that what had woken her was a surge of energy.

"Someone tried the wards," her mother explained. "I strengthened them. Rest."

Several days passed, and all was well. Whatever her mother did must have worked. The house was extremely well warded, and no attacks came.

Still, her mother sat all the girls down one Wednesday morning.

"We might need to go on a trip," she announced. Her eyes had dark circles under them. Vicky had never seen her mother look so tired.

"If there's another attack on the wards, we'll need to hide," her father added.

And Vicky was afraid.

"I can just go to the school," she offered.

"We don't know who is responsible," her mother said. "I hear even the court fears an attack now. You don't want to be there. And Corvus? Well, the headmaster has become part of a group of dangerous people."

Vicky nodded. She did not want to spend her life thinking about being attacked. They sort of *were*, though. They currently lived in their house with heavy wards and plans to flee.

"I don't want any of this," Vicky said. "Why does the world have to be so monstrous?"

"Monster!" yelled Alice. "No mons'ers!"

Lizzie tried to soothe her, but it was no use.

"Come on. Let's go make something to eat while Mama talks to Vicky," their dad said cheerily as Alice continued to fuss. "No monsters here, Alice. Or in the kitchen."

After her sisters left the room, Vicky's mother sat silently. Then she sighed and began to talk. "I had no plans to speak of this while you were so young, but things are unstable. I should tell you. You may have even guessed by now."

"Guessed what?"

"We are *very* related to the queen, Vicky. We are her only living relatives. The rest of our family is dead. It's just us. And her."

"I remember she called you 'cousin.'" Vicky stared at her mother in amazement. "You . . . you mean we really are *her* cousins? Is that why . . . I'm different? Am I . . . royalty?"

"You are. All royal heirs have gifts. Special strengths with wards and weapons. In the past, the strongest was to be heir. The next crowned."

"But that's you—you are the strongest!" Vicky said. The

thought of her mother as a *queen* was almost too much to consider. "And so . . . *you grew up a princess*? Why didn't you tell us? Shouldn't we know who we are?"

"I didn't grow up as royalty." Her mother pulled her closer and held her tightly. "My family died when I was about Alice's age. We were attacked, and Evangeline lived. Everyone thought I was dead, too, but Evangeline hid me."

"She didn't take you to the palace?"

"No." Her mother laughed, but it wasn't a joke. "I grew up somewhere *very* unlike a palace. My cousin sent me away to keep me safe . . . And I was anonymous—until I developed the gifts you have now. Then I was found and sent to Corvus. I'd be a threat to her unless I was serving her. And I served her well for many years. But that wasn't the life I wanted. I wanted a family. You, Vicky, and your sisters and father are all I need."

"But what happens if I can't hide my skills either?" Vicky thought of how easily ward work came to her. It was like breathing: she couldn't resist it sometimes. Blades came easily to her hand, and energy came quickly to her wards. She wasn't sure she'd ever be great at hiding either one.

"You have to," her mother said. "There are people who are a threat to us, Vicky Love. But as long as we keep to ourselves, no one will know what we are, and we can stay safe. She won't tell."

Suddenly, all of Vicky's desires—to be more, to have friends, to meet the queen—collapsed. These things, which she was only just beginning to want, were too dangerous.

To be safe, to protect her family, meant staying unnoticed.

CHAPTER 18

◆ ◆ ◆

Vicky

Aside from Vicky's restless sleep, everything seemed to settle down in the following weeks. No more messengers from the queen arrived. The house gargoyles brought no alarming reports.

Vicky asked her mom some important questions. "Who knows? Who can I trust?"

"Tik—my old friend who teaches at Corvus," she said. "Nightshade."

Vicky knew who the Nightshades were; everyone in the empire knew *that* name.

"The chimera," her mother added.

"The chimera?"

"Nightshade took me to the Netherwhere," her mother said. "It's a fantastic place. And the chimera, Ebba, was a marvel! Like the gargoyles, Ebba is always honest. Confusing sometimes—chimeras like riddles and have so many feelings about *everything*, but they are kind, too."

Vicky shook her head, but her mum laughed. "What a world, Vicky! To be friends with a chimera was a wondrous surprise. You can trust Nightshade *and* the chimera."

And her mother sounded more relaxed, so Vicky started to think everything was fine—right up to the night that Lizzie's screams woke her.

She was sleepwalking again when it happened. Vicky looked around, wondering where she was. In a blink, she realized she'd ended up in the library again. Her inability to stay where she'd been when she'd fallen asleep meant that she was not in the bedroom with Lizzie. It meant that she wasn't there with Lizzie when her second scream started—and was cut off suddenly.

The lesson they'd all been taught for as long as Vicky could remember was clear: if there ever was an Incident, the girls were to hide. They'd *sworn* on it. Vicky knew the rules, had sworn to uphold them, but . . . she couldn't. She grabbed the fire poker, which was almost as long as she was tall, and tiptoed to the door of the library.

She waited to hear the sounds of her sisters' voices, or fighting, or cries, but there was only silence. It stretched and unfurled like smoke, filling the air, until Vicky was sure that her heart would burst from fear.

The very thing that Vicky counted as normal in the darkest hours was now the thing that filled her with horror. Tonight, silence wasn't the sound of things being all right. It was the sound of things gone very, *very* wrong.

And when that terrible absence of sound seemed to grow

large enough to smother her, it became worse: Footsteps and thumps over her head told her that there were at least three unknown people in the house right now. Voices confirmed it.

There was no way that a small girl could overcome three grown people. Not alone. Not if her parents hadn't been able to do so.

Vicky walked back to the fireplace. Now she had to do what her parents had made her promise . . .

Hide until morning.

Wait until you are sure.

Not a peep, Vicky Love. Use the wards.

Vicky curled into a ball inside the empty fireplace, shivering in her thin nightdress and waiting, hoping against hope for her parents to come tell her that she was still dreaming. She stayed there until the morning light slipped in around the edges of the drapes.

"That was just a dream," she said to herself as she slowly got up. "A bad one. My sisters are fine. My parents are fine."

She forced herself to walk to the door and repeated these assurances silently to herself, in case there *were* strangers in the house. She slowly ascended the stairs, fire poker in hand. It wasn't a sword, but it would do in a pinch.

She prayed that everyone was fine as she gripped the glass knob on the door to her parents' bedroom.

When she stepped into the room to see both of her parents' unmoving forms, she bit her own hand to keep from screaming as her sisters had. She could tell without touching her parents that they were dead.

And she was certain that her whole family was gone, that they would never again be with her in this world.

It *was* a nightmare, but it was one she couldn't wake from.

There had been an Incident, and Vicky was the only one left alive.

With hands that were shaking, she went into the room and took the athame that was beside Mama's side of the bed. Mama hadn't worn it to sleep last night. That had been a mistake. Maybe she had thought the wards on the house were strong enough. Maybe she was finally so exhausted from weeks of being extra-alert that she had forgotten to wear it.

Vicky slid the small knife out of the holster and clutched it until she was hurting her hand. That pain meant she was awake. It meant this was real. Steadily, she drew a ward to hide herself, and then she walked back out of the room.

Vicky stayed as still as she could and tried to figure out what to do. She wasn't sure how long she sat in the hallway outside her bedroom, the fire poker across her legs and tears spilling down her face.

Midday came and passed, and still she sat in the silent house. There was no way she could make sense of the next thing she should be doing. She was sure there was such a thing, but she had no idea of what it could be.

She was still sitting in the same spot when she heard the sound of heavy footsteps ascending the stairs again. Everything Vicky had learned in her parents' years of lessons said she should run, but she couldn't leave her family.

The weight of her tears held her steady, unable to leave them. Vicky came to her feet and lifted the fire poker.

Let them come.

"Victoria?"

It wasn't until he spoke that she realized she'd let the ward drop. She wasn't hidden now, and the man standing in her house was staring at her, taking in her weapon and her wet cheeks. He was a polished sort, suit coat over his shirt and vest, walking cane with a handle carved into something she couldn't make out, and hat held in his other hand.

"You *are* Victoria, aren't you?" He peered at her from behind silver-framed glasses. "Twelve years this past summer. The middle child. You favor your mother."

"I don't know you."

"It's been many years since you've seen me—time flies by. Your parents were to meet me this morning. When they didn't come round the manor, I became concerned." He smiled, but it didn't make him look any more sincere. Her father had taught her how to read people's faces. He'd pointed out the ways people tightened their eyes or pressed their lips together when they lied, and explained that the best liars stared you straight in the eyes when they told you their mistruths.

This man was a good liar—or he was telling the truth.

"Are they here?" he asked.

Vicky pointed to the door. She'd left it cracked open, unable to look long at them but unable to close them away.

Silent moments passed while the man went into her

parents' room and then her sisters' room. *My room.* Vicky couldn't go in there. She'd wanted to, but she hadn't been able to make herself do so. She hoped the man would come back out and say they were fine or even have her sisters at his side.

Instead, when he came back, he seemed shaken. All he said was, "You'll come with me, Victoria. I'll send the authorities to deal with this."

"No."

"You are just a child," he said calmly. "I will handle this. It's what they'd have wanted."

"No."

"I am your Uncle Albert, Victoria. You're my responsibility now."

He walked away, and for a few moments, she hoped he was gone for good. The main door opened and closed. Relief filled her, but it was a brief thing. She heard him returning, and soon there were others. More strangers filled her home. Some of them were Ravens; those were the only ones she could stand to look at for more than a moment. She didn't *trust* them, but she recognized a few of them who had visited her parents. More importantly, their eyes didn't lie. Their sorry looks and kind smiles were real.

Grief was harder to fake than many things.

One of them, a woman, brought her clothes. Another brought her food and sat with her in silence as she tried to eat.

Then they were all gone, and she was left with Albert and an official from Queen Evangeline's palace. He wore the royal badge on his stiff red uniform.

"Albert Sweeney has accepted responsibility for you," the

court officer said. "He's graciously agreed to look after you until you reach your majority. Your parents' estate will be held in trust for you, but Mr. Sweeney has expressed that he'd rather not use that for your upkeep. He'll support you."

"No." It seemed like the only word Vicky could say.

Only moments later, Uncle Millicent settled outside the window. He bowed his head and ground out, "Mistress."

It was true, she was the mistress of the house. She blinked, tears blurring her vision.

"The whole family is dead," she said softly.

"Not all of you," Uncle Millicent said.

Vicky wasn't sure that the reminder that she survived was a comfort. She didn't want to be in this world alone. But the gargoyle flew away, and Vicky was left standing silent with a stranger.

"Come, Victoria. There is nothing left for you here." Albert took her elbow and propelled her toward the door.

Vicky stiffened and jerked away.

"For those of us sworn to our queen's command as your parents were, as *I* am, there are always risks." He paused and waited for her to meet his eyes. "There can also be justice."

This time there was no hint of a lie in his expression.

"Would you like that, Victoria? To avenge them? To take the things they taught you and one day learn enough to be a force of justice?"

The emptiness that had been trying to smother her since that first scream vanished at his words. Someone had taken her family, her life, and she wanted to *hurt* them. Surely, that would make her feel better.

"I can help you," he said.

Vicky brushed her skirt down carefully, tucked her hair behind her ears, and softly said, "Then, Uncle Albert, I will go with you."

She would figure out how to avenge her family—even if that meant that she had to be a Raven first.

Part II

CHAPTER 19

∘────◇────∘

Rupert

Seeing a bad thing and not being able to stop it was the worst. Kat was gone, and this time, Rupert was sure he was weeping. He couldn't comfort the children or fix this, so he did the next best thing.

"Albert!"

"How did you . . . ?" Albert Sweeney was a large man, rather like an enormous badger. He stood in his study, glaring at the shattered window where Rupert had entered, and in the moment between arrival and clarity, he looked terrified. He knew enough about the world to know they'd had a loss.

"Who?"

"Kat."

It was all that Rupert needed to say. Sweeney had moved as quickly as his badger-like shape ever did, and Rupert was grateful that he'd go look after Vicky Love. Sweeney and Kat had grown apart when she'd started her family. But Rupert knew that Sweeney still loved Kat, despite how they'd argued the last few times they'd met.

Like all of the children-who-were-grown, Sweeney had to deal with his duty to the empire.

With another tug of the ley line energy, Rupert was gone toward Glass City. The ley lines were how gargoyles tracked people. He could find them in the stream of magic that flowed in the earth. If he'd known who was coming to hurt Kat, he could have watched for them, but there were countless men and women who served the Glass Queen and the collective of court leaders.

Rupert couldn't track them all.

And so he'd failed her.

Rupert landed with a less-than-graceful thump in the room where Tik was, as always, it seemed, practicing. He practiced almost as much now as when he was on missions for the queen.

"Kat," he told Tik.

The grown-up version of the boy bowed his head, as if the pain was too much. After a moment in which he made a noise that sounded more like the boy he once was, Tik lifted his now-wet face and said, "Wilbur?"

"Gone."

"Who did it?" Tik asked. "The queen—or her enemies?"

Rupert had no answers. The ways of humans and their drive for power and wealth confused him.

"Tell Sweeney and Nightshade," Tik said, hand tightening on his sword.

The scream of rage Tik released as Rupert left him made the gargoyle feel like he weighed more than a gargoyle could. That feeling, grief, made everything seem dim. Kat was gone.

All that was left was to watch over those who remained.

With that thought in mind, Rupert flew toward Nightshade Manor.

CHAPTER 20

◆———◆———◆

Vicky

Vicky was hazy on the details of arriving at Uncle Albert's estate. She knew that her heart ached like she'd been the one pierced by a knife. She knew that there weren't any tears left in her eyes to cry.

She looked around and thought that the house in front of her was big enough for daylong games of hide-and-seek with her sisters.

But that was *before*.

This was *after*.

They were gone. She was alone. They were gone because of who they were.

Was it the queen? Had she ordered this?

"I know it is hard to believe, but someday you will recover. I have lost people, too, and I promise you, time will ease this pain," Uncle Albert said.

Vicky was about to object when a pitiful howl drew her attention. In the corner of the room, sprawled out on a giant pillow, was a basset hound with the biggest, saddest eyes she'd ever seen.

"Billingsly," Uncle Albert said. "He's a surly old boy."

The dog heaved himself off his cushion and strolled over to them. Then he plopped down and stared up at Vicky. His saggy jowls and overlong ears drooped back, making him look even funnier than he already did.

"You can take him to your room," Uncle Albert offered. "You could both use someone to cuddle."

Tears filled Vicky's eyes again. As far as she knew, she'd never met Billingsly—or Uncle Albert—before. But they were what she had now.

She dropped to the floor, pulled the surprisingly heavy dog into a hug, and buried her face against his fur. It was a small thing—a hug—but it felt large.

Albert patted her shoulder absently. "Very good."

A woman in a stiff dark-red dress and white apron walked into the foyer. She bowed. "Miss Victoria's rooms are ready. Some of her things are here, too."

Vicky stayed on the floor with the slobbering dog.

"Go with Rebecca, Victoria. She'll see you—and Billingsly—to your rooms and collect you for breakfast in the morning."

It was too early to sleep normally, but she'd hardly slept the night before. Sleep sounded perfect, except for the regular fear of sleepwalking—and the new terror of seeing the faces of her dead family in her dreams.

Uncle Albert must have seen her hesitation, because he

added, "I have a mild calming tonic for you to take tonight. Rebecca will give it to you."

Mutely, Vicky stood and looked at Rebecca.

"Come, Billingsly." Rebecca ordered, and then she, too, was silent as she led Vicky and the dog down a long corridor.

When the older woman pushed open the door, Vicky looked at the room with as much interest as she'd given the little bit of the house she'd already seen. It was a perfectly fine room. A massive four-poster bed was slightly off-center in the middle of the room. Dark-red drapes—the exact color of Rebecca's uniform—surrounded it, hanging so that their thick fringe brushed the floor. The drapes were pulled back at the corners, but if the night were cold, they could be unfastened to block the air.

Alice had loved beds like this.

Tears blurred Vicky's eyes again, and she couldn't see the rest of the room clearly through them.

"Drink this." From her apron, Rebecca withdrew a vial filled with a green syrup. It wasn't the worst-looking medicine Vicky had ever taken, although the smell of it when uncorked was unpleasant.

Again, Vicky obeyed. As Rebecca helped her get undressed and tucked her into bed, the medicine began to take effect. A moment later, Vicky felt the *thump* of Billingsly lying down on the mattress next to her.

"Rest," Rebecca told her.

It was a sleeping draft of some strength, more powerful than any Vicky had ever taken. Her mother had given her several such drafts to try to help her stop sleepwalking. None of them had been this strong.

When Rebecca bent and brushed Vicky's hair back from her face, Vicky could almost pretend it was Mama's voice whispering, "Poor dear."

Vicky wrapped her arm around Billingsly and pretended that the dog's steady breathing was Lizzie's. His fur didn't help that illusion, but the medicine was already pulling her into sleep.

CHAPTER 21

❖——◇——❖

Algernon

Algernon slipped out of the Nightshade house early the next morning. These few hours were his treasure, and he hated that they were about to end. There was a postscript to the weekly chores list, simply noting:

Algernon to start school. Should pack.

Before the ragged boys were up, before there were business calls for his father, before life resumed, there was only the quiet. In the peaceful hours, Algernon could be someone else. He could pretend that he was a boy with a real family and a mother of his own.

He let himself out of the house, the door closing so quietly that not even the young thief napping in the foyer heard it. Sometimes the act of sneaking around his house felt like a test, and knowing his father, it probably was. Still, Algernon took pride in his stealth as he wound his way down the twisting path to the largest of the alchemical gardens. This was the garden with the fewest venomous plants and prickling things, where Algernon often felt at peace.

But not this morning.

"Father?"

"Algernon." That was it, the whole reply, a terse naming of him.

"Were there ingredients you needed?" he asked the man.

His father turned around, and Algernon was surprised not to find either glass or basket in his hands. More surprising still, his hands were ungloved. When Algernon saw that, he asked, "Are you unwell?"

"I was thinking," his father said. "I used to do that out here in the gardens, back before you boys came. Now I see you out here many mornings."

"Oh."

"I thought it better to leave the space to you than to try to share it," his father said. "Wasn't really sure what was best, you know. Parenting was never something I aspired to." He paused and smiled a sad smile. "Neither was alchemy."

Algernon looked at him curiously. His father had never spoken to him like this.

Algernon followed his father along the flagstone path further into the garden. The plants stretched in so many directions that it was a meditative experience to follow their lines with his gaze, like untangling vast knots. There was something almost magical about being here with the flora when it was still in its natural state, before it became the stuff of cures and poisons, of medicinals and venoms.

"There are things about our role in this world that you don't like either. I am aware of that," his father said as Algernon caught up to him.

"I know that the queen's decisions are final," Algernon allowed. "And leaving her service is deadly."

"Yes. No one has done it, you know. There were people who tried. A couple. Friends of mine, but they are dead now, too," his father said. "And the queen insists that Alistair will receive every training you do. If you die at school, he'll become the next Master Nightshade."

"Even though I'm having to go a *year* early, I won't die doing something as simple as taking classes," Algernon said.

"After all of your trips to the Netherwhere, I should hope not," his father said pointedly.

Algernon's jaw dropped.

"Of course I know you visit. I haven't been in years," his father continued. "They are not fond of our queen there, and I'm marked too much by her at this stage. But do give Ebba my greetings . . . They last told me I would be eaten if I returned 'smelling of the palace and lies,'" his father added blithely. "I don't think I'd like being eaten . . ."

"So, I'll lose the Netherwhere?" Algernon managed to ask.

His father looked away. "I did, but . . . one never truly knows. Best not to let anyone know you are able to go there at all."

They stood in the garden, surrounded by the tools of the trade they were both born into, and Algernon thought again about how he didn't truly know his father. They shared blood, a fate, and a house, but they were still strangers.

"You have questions," his father said. "Go ahead."

"Why the orphans? There aren't *that* many tasks that need done around here."

His father smiled, looking remarkably like Alistair for a moment, before saying, "My best friend at Corvus started out as a thief. She was my first actual friend. When I arrived there, I had no idea how to speak to other children. I had no brothers. My older brother died before I was old enough to know him. You see, I was the spare. I'd never *met* other children until school."

"So, you brought thieves home so we would know how to make friends?" Algernon asked incredulously.

His father shrugged. "That—and there aren't many options for children without families. Our orphanages are awful, and . . . we have the space. And when the boys leave, they have skills that they learned from the Queen's Alchemist. I give them each a letter to take if they want to secure a position as a lab worker or assistant."

Algernon stared at his father. He'd been treating their home as if it were an orphanage for thieves. He wasn't trying to *use* the thieves. He was trying to *help* them. He was rescuing them one by one, and Algernon hadn't even realized it.

Master Nightshade continued. "If I could have chosen a sister, I'd have chosen my thief friend. She talked about living in the thieves' houses and how much easier Corvus was because of it. She could move through places I couldn't because of them . . . And she sometimes talked about what she might have done differently if she'd had choices other than Corvus. I bring home the ones that remind me of her best traits."

"Do you still talk to her?"

At that, Master Nightshade breathed a little more rapidly, and then calmly said, "She's dead."

"I'm sor—"

"That reminds me, there will be a student at Corvus you'll need to watch," his father said. "I can't say more yet, but the queen wants Victoria Wardrop to be closely monitored. She's selected you to do it. Your first task for her."

Something in his father's voice made Algernon certain that there was more to the task.

"Must I?" he said.

His father grabbed his arm tightly. "Algernon, you will do whatever the queen wants. You'll be the Queen's Alchemist, but sometimes she asks other things of us." His father's grip loosened, and some of the fear in his voice seemed to recede as he continued. "I was terrified, too, when your grandfather started telling me of my duties. But those who disobey die. It's that simple."

His father's intensity seemed unusual, so Algernon asked, "Is that what happened to your Raven friend? The thief?"

When his father answered, his voice sounded like he was choking, and all he said was, "Yes."

"So, I'm to watch this girl," Algernon prompted after a moment.

"Victoria. Help her if she needs it. Keep me updated if anything that happens seems peculiar, especially if it seems cruel or dangerous."

Algernon stared at his father, wondering exactly what chaos they were facing. "At *Corvus*? Isn't cruel or dangerous rather relative there?"

"You'll know."

"And how will I tell you? Will you be visiting me or something?"

His father looked weary. "No need for me to visit. I'll be teaching there."

"*Teaching?*"

"Alchemical Arts," Master Nightshade said. "Her Majesty asks that I be at the school while you and Victoria are there. I agreed." He paused and added, "Be wary of the headmaster, Algernon. Tell Victoria the same. Her parents died recently, so she has no one else to warn her."

Algernon wanted to ask if her parents were his friends, the Ravens who died.

"The headmaster?" he asked instead. "Why a warning about him?"

"The queen came to power when she was just a child," his father said. "So a group called the Collective was put in place to guide her. The headmaster has become their leader, and Her Majesty would like me there at Corvus." He sighed. "Nightshades serve the queen, Algernon. Our loyalty is absolute."

Algernon didn't understand all of it, but he figured out that neither the queen nor his father trusted the headmaster. He felt like there were a lot of other things his father wasn't saying, but Algernon needed to deal with other, more immediate things first. "What about Alistair and the boys who are *here*? Who will feed them and watch out for them?"

The look on his father's face made it perfectly clear that he hadn't thought of that. He was used to Algernon looking after practical things.

His father frowned. "Well, I suppose I can send a letter to Her Majesty's office. I'm sure they'll hire a suitable caretaker, or . . . whatever the title is for someone who can take care of them." He stared at a flowering bellaglove—a hybrid of foxglove and belladonna that Algernon's grandfather had created—and added, "We depart in a month. You, me, and Milan."

"Milan?"

"He's able to read," the alchemist said. "Has been reading my potions. So I thought we could educate him. It's either that or kill him."

"Corvus seems like a better choice," Algernon agreed.

"Let us hope," the man said.

CHAPTER 22

◆——◆——◆

Vicky

The next couple of weeks were a blur to Vicky. She was trying to keep from grieving, but it was only with the help of calming elixirs that she could manage anything at all.

The house was far too large for so few people, and Vicky wandered through the drafty rooms in silence. Reading became the only way she could almost forget for a few moments. Albert nodded at her from time to time. The wheezing dog curled heavily against her throughout the long hours. And Vicky learned not to weep quite as much or as loudly.

She began to plan. First, she needed to figure out who was responsible for destroying her family. Was the queen behind it? Her mother had never trusted the queen, but then again her mother didn't trust *most* people. Was it someone else? Why did her parents dislike the headmaster of Corvus? Was Vicky safe now?

When Vicky had met her, the queen had warned that there were dangers.

Maybe she should go see her—or would that be betraying

Mama? Maybe she should make her way to Glass City and get her swords from the fearless blacksmith. Maybe she should find Ebba, the chimera her mother had liked so much. Or Nightshade, the alchemist. Or Tik, the sword master at Corvus—which was also where the headmaster lived.

There were so many questions and dangers that Vicky felt lost. All she knew for sure was that she had to work until she found the answers.

Then she would somehow make sure the killers got sent to the royal dungeons until they were as sorrow-filled as she was.

But first, she needed to stop weeping and feeling so hollow. Food tasted like sand and felt like it would choke her. Her eyes were raw from tears and the frequent waking terrors. Grief was weighing her down.

That night, she went to the massive library in her uncle's house to ask for more elixir, but a stranger sat alongside Uncle Albert. As Vicky entered the room, he rose to his feet. Uncle Albert did as well.

"May I present Victoria Sweeney," Uncle Albert said.

Vicky tensed. That hadn't been her surname before, and she didn't like the change. But maybe it would be easier to hide at Corvus with a different name.

"Victoria, this is Master Nightshade," he continued.

Her mother had said she could trust Nightshade. In her mind, she'd imagined him to look more like Poppa, muscles and stealth, but the man in the library resembled a cross between an alley dog and a hunting bird.

"Your mother was a friend," Master Nightshade said in a greeting of sorts.

"I know." Vicky folded her hands together tightly, as if it would keep them from shaking. "She mentioned you."

"You look like Kat, but you have Wilbur's eyes," the man continued. "Could see right through the slightest misdirection, that one."

She wasn't sure of the decorum for meeting the queen's chief poisoner or for talking about her parents. She assumed he knew that they were dead, but he was speaking about them so comfortably that Vicky didn't know what to do or say. Maybe death was easier for a man who made poisons.

Uncle Albert cleared his throat, drawing Master Nightshade's attention to him.

"Right, then," the poisoner said. "I was asked to bring a treatment here to offer you. It's stronger than the calmer you've been taking, longer-lasting too. I've administered it previously to many people—usually adults, though."

He fumbled around in his pockets until he pulled out a series of vials. They were all different: one the color of clouds before a storm, another the hue of angry seas, a third as black as the most expensive ink.

Master Nightshade met her eyes again. "I won't give you the treatment without your consent. I have too much regard for your parents."

"What will it do?"

"Remove your grief. But it will remove your shadow—and your emotions, too," he explained with the bluntness she'd occasionally heard when her parents had spoken where they thought the girls wouldn't hear them.

"Does it hurt?"

"Yes," the alchemist said. "It's a dark business, taking your shadow. Dark things hurt."

"But it'll make me stop feeling like this?"

"It will, but so will *time*. The intensity of what you are feeling will pass without potions. You can just wait. It will get easier."

Vicky couldn't imagine this horrible pain getting easier. She couldn't imagine waiting.

"I want to stop the pain *now*," she said. "I want to find the people who hurt my family and . . . do something. But I can't go to school or learn if I'm waking up screaming and too angry and tired to study. I have decided that I will be a Raven. Like my parents. And I will find the people who took my family."

She couldn't quite say "killed." That word hurt like daggers in her belly. She could tell that Uncle Albert and Master Nightshade knew what she meant, though.

The alchemist lined up the three vials of medicine he'd withdrawn from his pockets. "This will stop your pain."

She hesitated briefly, a panicked fear coming to her so strongly that she wanted to choke. "I'll remember everything. Right? I need to remember them, the way they were, the way I felt. Swear to me that this doesn't make me feel better by making me *forget*."

Master Nightshade smiled sadly and then said, "I could make you forget, but this isn't that sort of treatment. Everything you know or feel up to this moment will still be within you."

Vicky held out a hand for the first vial.

As if it were a signal of some sort, Uncle Albert stood and began to open all of the drapes in the room. He paused at the door to throw the lock, then glanced at Master Nightshade.

The poisoner uncorked the vial of cloud-gray liquid and held it out to her. "When Albert has finished letting in the light, you'll need to drink the next one. We need it bright enough to see your whole shadow. Sit. Take this now."

With a shaking hand, Vicky accepted the vial.

She sat on the sofa across from Master Nightshade and lifted the vial to her lips. She drank it in one swallow. It felt like clouds were sliding into her body, cotton wrapping around her sore heart and muffling the terror and grief she'd felt since her sister's scream woke her.

As she leaned back into the pillows of the sofa, Vicky felt boneless. She wasn't tired, though. She was more alert than she'd ever been.

"Can you go faster?" Master Nightshade asked.

He was looking behind himself, where Uncle Albert was lighting candle after candle. The room was brighter by the moment. Vicky watched as he lit several more candles. The room was growing so bright that she could barely keep her eyes open. It hurt to do so.

"Last one." Uncle Albert's voice came from across the room.

At the same time, a vial was pressed into her hand.

"Swallow," Master Nightshade ordered. His hand was on her forehead, tilting her head back.

The medicine slid down her throat—and as it did, her body felt as if it had been freed from some invisible weight. There was a seam on her body she'd never known to exist before.

She couldn't see it, but she knew it was there. Attached at the seam was something weightless. It stretched over her like her entire body was coated in something slick that was a part of her.

"You're sure about this, Victoria?" the poisoner asked. He had the third vial, the ink-black one, in his hand. "This will wear off if we stop now."

"My family was murdered." Vicky's voice was remarkably steady, and no tears filled her eyes. As promised, her emotions were dulled by the treatment. "I want to avenge them . . . And my mother said to trust you."

Master Nightshade shot a look at Uncle Albert, who looked as sad as Billingsly usually did, before staring at her and explaining, "This will *hurt*. Most people who tried it were insensible from the pain."

Vicky extended her hand.

"I'm sorry for your loss," Master Nightshade said. He uncorked and handed her the third vial.

Vicky felt her grief try to come back, but she snatched the vial and swallowed the alchemical potion down in one long drink.

She heard the glass drop from her fingers and shatter on the floor. The garment on her body, that slick shape that coated her, was now clinging to her like it was made up of millions of tiny teeth. Each tooth had sunk into her skin at once. The garment—which she now understood was her actual shadow—didn't want to be torn from her. She didn't know how to tell it that she wanted this, didn't know how to let a part of her *self* know that she wanted to be free of it. She couldn't tell her hand or her heart that she wanted to be rid of them, but this, this inky, wet part of her, she could surrender. She just didn't know how to make it let go.

The teeth sank deeper, and she felt her body start to shake all over.

She heard Uncle Albert say, "Keep her steady." His voice seemed like it was years away, echoing down a hall that didn't exist.

And then she felt a tearing, as if every bit of her skin was being tugged away from her body at once—and her shadow bit harder still. Neither body nor shadow wanted this.

Vicky turned her head at the footsteps approaching, and when she did, she saw Uncle Albert with an upraised sword.

The thought that he was a monster she shouldn't have trusted filled her mind just as the sword descended and sliced deep into the cushion beside her. As the blade's edge pushed through the beautiful leather, Master Nightshade gripped her by both arms and yanked her forward, pulling her to her feet and off the chair.

There, on the leather cushion, she could see the inky shape of her body. It squirmed and kicked, as if it could reach her, and she reached her hand toward it.

"Stop," Master Nightshade said.

She looked at him. Her body felt unsteady, like her sense of balance was pinned to the leather along with her shadow, but she stumbled away from both the alchemist and the part of herself that she'd had removed. She stared at the dark form, wondering if it would die, if she had hurt it. "It looks like it's in pain."

"Shadows have no skin, so they don't feel pain," Uncle Albert said.

Master Nightshade added, "It's you, Vicky. Do *you* hurt?"

For a moment, she hesitated, trying to feel everything, trying to discover any pains that were hidden under the potions. All she felt was a vast sea of calmness, as if she had been submerged into some new sort of silence, where answers were things to pluck out of the waveless waters.

"No, I don't."

The alchemist stared at her and prompted, "What do you feel? What emotions are you experiencing?"

Victoria smiled. "Nothing. I feel nothing at all."

CHAPTER 23

Milan

Milan was glad to return to Glass City. He looked out the carriage window as they rolled toward the school. He was surprised to be inside rather than on top, but the alchemist had simply given him a shove toward the door when he'd started to ascend to the roof. And Milan went with it.

Somewhere in the crowds were the people he used to know—and he felt like he'd come home but found that the door was locked. It wasn't that the thieves would no longer accept him, but they wouldn't understand why he was going to school. His love of learning and of books was something many of the thieves had mocked.

Milan didn't care much about being a Raven, but he wanted to *learn*. He wanted to be something other than one of the rare old thieves who had survived the streets and created a house. The odds of growing old were low for a thief. For a boy whose biggest dream had been surviving and owning a few books, the possibilities that Corvus offered were too big to comprehend.

For now, Milan was just happy to be back in Glass City. He'd missed it. The sounds of confusion and crowds were like music in the city. Voices lifted in anger and joy, calling out warnings and greetings. Wheels clattered over uneven streets. It was home.

The brief time at Nightshade Manor had been fine, but it wasn't the same kind of peace as the chaos of the city. The open spaces of the country still felt dangerous in ways that the familiar closeness of the city didn't.

Or maybe it was simply knowing where to look for dangers.

"Is this where you learned to steal?" Algernon blurted out.

"The city?"

"Here." Algernon gestured at the area around them.

It wasn't good pickings, too many people with empty pockets.

Milan shook his head. "Not *right* here."

"Will we pass it?"

The alchemist ignored them—or was lost inside his own thoughts. He was often so distracted that he had no idea what was happening around him. The lab had been on fire at least twice without the alchemist noticing.

"No, we won't be anywhere near my old haunts," Milan said.

Both of the Nightshades stared out opposite windows after that, and by the time the carriage arrived at the school, it had been well over an hour of silence. The sound of a stranger greeting them was very welcome—even if it was only Master Nightshade who was greeted.

"We were starting to think you'd changed your mind, Nightshade. You were to be here several days ago." The woman smiled with the sort of chill than would make pickpockets and highwaymen flinch. She had an assortment of enormous feathers jabbed into her towering hair, and her eyes were flat and cold, like a swamp serpent who had spotted a meal.

The alchemist muttered something Milan didn't catch, and the woman made a quick gesture with an athame before pivoting on one foot and walking away. She was several yards away before she said, "The children are both in House Valentinus, since the ragged child isn't a legacy."

Milan assumed this "house" business must be similar to which thieves' den one belonged to on the streets.

"Your manners are worse than a wet goat's, Agatha," Master Nightshade called out, and she turned back and lifted a hand as if to strike him from a distance.

"Valentinus is almost entirely alchemists," Algernon explained quietly to Milan. "There are other houses: Szabo is mostly spies, Ophelia is ward workers, and Talhoffer is combat. Invictus is the legacy house, for the ones related to or sponsored by Ravens and other former students."

Master Nightshade made a sour face before glancing back at the boys and explaining, "Invictus are already connected to powerful people. You'll find no easy allies there, but the Szabos and Ophelias have their uses. Make allies there."

"And Talhoffer?" Milan prompted.

Instead of answering, Nightshade turned his back and told the driver, "Bring the bags inside." Then he glanced at the boys as if he'd suddenly remembered their presence and told them, "I shouldn't have insulted goats."

Algernon glanced at Milan.

He shrugged. He wasn't sure what to think of the feathered woman or the grumpy alchemist. People were strange.

They followed Master Nightshade to the door. Milan tried to ignore the way that every gargoyle along the ledge turned to stare at them. They'd barely noticed him when he'd lived in the streets of Glass City. Now, however, their gazes followed the boys until they crossed out of the open atrium and stepped inside a passage.

When the door they'd entered through closed with a loud crash, Algernon jumped.

"Too much time in gardens and muck," the feather-wearing woman said snidely.

"Better that than too much time failing to be clever," his father replied lightly.

"He'll get no kindness from *me* for being a teacher's son," she said pointedly. "You being here . . . at the same time as your son. It's bad form, Nightshade."

"We all have our orders," he said. "Would you like me to send word that you question the orders?"

The woman startled at that, a look of fear crossing her face. "Of course not! But that doesn't explain"—she waved at Milan and pursed her lips—"bringing one of your orphans."

By this point, Master Nightshade was humming softly, as if he couldn't hear her. He paused and announced, "The lab and gardens have been kept up, I expect, but I will need to inspect them."

Then he walked away.

The boys exchanged another look, and then Algernon asked, "Where is House Valentinus?"

She leveled a glare at them that might've made the boys quake if they were different people. Milan had lived on the streets; Algernon had been raised to be the Queen's Alchemist. They'd both been to the Netherwhere. They could face a teacher with a bad attitude.

"It's late, and we have studying to do," Algernon said.

Milan spoke then. "Agatha—"

"*Lady* Agatha, thief. You will give me my title."

Algernon said, "How would we know that was—"

"If you were worthy of being here, you'd know," Lady Agatha said curtly, marching ahead of them.

The boys looked at each other and shrugged. They followed her till they reached a massive steel door.

"If you're bright enough to get inside, you can sleep in beds," Lady Agatha announced before spinning on her heel and stomping away.

The door was covered with a series of gears, pulleys, and locks. There were easily seven mechanical puzzles that were made up by the apparatus.

"What's the red stuff?" Milan asked.

Algernon looked where he was pointing. There, at the top of the door, was a small vial. If they didn't set all the clockwork pieces in place correctly, the vial would tilt.

"Liquid fire," Algernon said, scanning the area carefully as he answered.

"Heard of it, but . . . what is it?"

"It's dragon's . . . um . . . when they visit the bathroom." Algernon seemed more uncomfortable now than he had in the Netherwhere facing strange dangerous creatures.

Milan laughed. "Figure out the puzzle or get dragon sh—"

"*Urine*," Algernon said quickly. "Not the other. It's liquid."

"That can be liquid, too. After a few of the things you and your brother tried to cook at the house, I can tell you for sure that—"

"Stop!" Algernon rubbed his cheeks as if it would make them less red and told Milan, "We can't use words like you were saying, not if there's a chance of being one of the Queen's Ravens."

Milan stopped laughing as quickly as he'd started. "Is that what you want?"

"It doesn't matter what I want. My father is Aloysius Nightshade. I'm his heir. That means I do a good job, learn, and become his replacement, or I die. If *that* happens, my brother will be stuck as his replacement. That's it. There are no other options for the eldest Nightshade."

Milan shook his head, but he didn't say anything.

Algernon looked away and studied the puzzle. "The first one is easy."

He lined up the tines of two gears so they caught. Milan could see that they'd propel the larger of the two gears counterclockwise when the latch of the handle was depressed. That would raise a lever.

Milan gestured at the lever in question. "It has to depress that switch."

"Which releases the copper-plated gear over there." Algernon pointed. "But is it to catch the small brass one or . . ."

"The other copper one," Milan finished. "See? It sets the chain loose over there."

They finished the puzzle far faster than Milan had expected, and once all the pieces were lined up, he pushed Algernon away and grabbed the handle quickly.

The mechanisms each clicked into place as they watched. At the top of the door, the vial of liquid fire shivered as if it might tilt, but instead it slid into a small keyhole.

With one last loud click, the door unlatched.

"Welcome to House Valentinus," a girl's voice said as the door swung inward. "I'm Meredith."

Milan stared at the girl. She didn't have the normal sunken eyes of someone who spent hours in a lab. She looked more like the gardening sort of alchemist—the sort Milan would rather be. Collecting ingredients with Algernon had been fun, especially when they went to the Netherwhere.

"Do you both speak the common tongue?" The girl had a haughty way about her that said she was somehow looking down at you even though she was the same height.

Milan nodded. "Which door for our rooms?"

Meredith folded her arms over her chest and glared. "I said, *I'm Meredith*."

Algernon managed to squeak out, "Pleased to meet you, Meredith."

As soon as he did so, she curtsied, and Algernon bowed stiffly in response.

With a slightly friendlier smile, Meredith walked over to Milan and repeated, "I'm Meredith."

Milan cleared his throat and mimicked what Algernon had done. "Pleased to see you, Meredith."

"*Meet* me," she corrected as she curtsied, but not as deeply as she had in front of Algernon. "Now, bow."

Awkwardly, he did so.

Meredith stared at them, and for a brief moment, she looked kind. "They'll eat you alive here if you're that easily intimidated. We'll work on that, so you don't disgrace our house."

Milan scowled. He wasn't *intimidated*. He simply didn't know the rules for talking to scary girls. Or bowing. Or the words that were expected.

He shouldn't be here.

Meredith shook her head at them and gestured. "You're to the left. Girls are always on the *right*," she said, before heading toward the door on the right. "First meal is at sunup here. If you're not at the dining hall on time, there is no food until midday meal."

Algernon was already opening the door to the bedchamber. It looked a lot like the nursery at Nightshade Manor, with rows of identical beds lining the wall.

Milan shut the door and walked to the bed where his newly acquired trunk was. He touched it, still not quite trusting that it was real. He had enough *things* now to need a proper trunk to carry them in.

"What was that all about?" he asked, gesturing toward the common room. He might not have known what to say to nob girls, but Nightshade ought to have known.

"She's a *girl*," Algernon said in a loud whisper.

Milan stared at Algernon. "So?"

"I've only seen them from the carriage a few times, and there were a few in the woods one day." Algernon paused, frowning. "And now I need to *watch* one of them, too."

"Meredith?"

Algernon shook his head. "No. The girl I'm to watch is called Victoria."

Milan squashed down a hope that the Victoria whom Algernon was supposed to watch was the same one he'd met in Skinner's Close. Surely, Victoria Wardrop wasn't here. Her parents were the only people ever to leave the Ravens, so they wouldn't send their daughter here, would they?

Milan sat down on his bed. It was the same as all the others—as if *he* were the same, too. He tried not to stare in shock at the empty beds. A common thief who had stolen, possibly from the families of the very people he'd sleep next to, was here, at the most secretive school in the empire.

CHAPTER 24

Victoria

Victoria stood at the massive window at Uncle Albert's house and stared out at the rain. The sound was soothing. It felt like an average rainy day of the sort she used to know—except she was Victoria Sweeney now. She was a girl in a lovely house about to set off to school. Without her messy emotions, Vicky could truly pretend that she was simply a girl who was excited to start the Corvus School for the Artfully Inclined.

The truth, in that way that truths often were, was complicated. She was also a girl who would avenge her parents one day. She was also a girl who was related to the queen. She was not an ordinary girl on an ordinary day. Perhaps no one was really ordinary.

"Do you have your good parasol?"

"Yes, Uncle Albert."

"Books?"

"*On Violence* by Howard the Hairless," she answered.

"*Alchemy* by Archimedes Nightshade, *Wards and When to Use Them* with my mother's notes in it, and her copy of *Argument Moste Foule* by Ethel of the Wild Highland Plains."

"Riding boots?" He frowned at her, so briefly that it was nothing more than a twitch. "The *new* ones, Victoria, not those ragged things."

The ragged boots had been Lizzie's. Wearing them made Victoria feel braver. "Both pairs are in my trunks."

Uncle Albert's frown returned. "Corvus is very selective, Victoria. Not just anyone can attend, and being admitted doesn't guarantee success."

Victoria nodded, but her opinion no longer mattered. *Vicky* had opinions. Vicky had laughed. Vicky had a family. Victoria had none of that. As Victoria, she had a *mission*. She would become the hidden knife, a weapon unexpected until it was drawn, and she'd find out who took her family and deliver the justice they deserved.

Uncle Albert sighed, seeming almost as wheezy as his old basset hound.

"I've packed what I'll be taking, and I'll be ready at half past three," she announced.

He nodded.

"Do you know a chimera?" Victoria asked quietly.

Uncle Albert frowned. "There is no such creature in our world."

Victoria quirked a brow at him. "Do you question my mother, Uncle?"

"*She* spoke of one?"

Victoria shrugged.

"Then it's over in the Netherwhere," he said. "Kat must have gone there sometime with Nightshade."

Victoria nodded. It sounded very much like Master Nightshade was the man to see—and alone this time.

Uncle Albert was giving her a home, but that wasn't the same as being trustworthy. Sometimes she trusted Albert Sweeney, and other times she reminded herself that she had no proof that he had been a true friend to her parents. Maybe her mother hadn't been wrong to be suspicious of almost everyone. Victoria had more questions than answers, and sometimes she thought that might be all she'd ever have.

SEVERAL HOURS LATER, Victoria stood beside Uncle Albert as he lifted the head of his walking stick and rapped it on the door to the school, as if reaching out with his hand to the door knocker was simply too much effort.

A woman with thick spectacles and an array of feathers in her hair opened the door. "Sweeney!"

"Agatha," he said, stepping forward, using the motion and his size to encourage her to back up.

The door thudded shut behind them.

The woman stared at Victoria a little longer than was polite. Victoria felt her presence, the skin-too-tight hum of ward work, and knew she was being read and studied. Vicky would've deflected that intrusion, but Victoria couldn't be modest about her abilities. Not now. She stood and consciously dropped her barriers.

Let them all know. She was going to excel here. Getting the queen's attention, her enemies' attention, *any* attention, was a risk she could take, now that she was attending Corvus.

"You'll do, girl. You'll do just fine. I am Lady Agatha." She turned away and crossed the vast, empty foyer. An enormous bustle at the back of her skirt made her bottom look almost like a velvet dining room chair.

Victoria followed, with Uncle Albert at her side. The octagonal foyer was the most boring room she'd ever seen. The ceiling was several stories high, but there were only layered glass windows to let in a dim light.

Lady Agatha reached a seemingly solid wall on the far side of the foyer and pressed on a panel, which prompted a click. In the next moments, a mechanical whirring began and a section of wall slid open. It was a strange mix of mechanized magic and handmade craftsmanship. The panels had runes etched in them, but they weren't ones Victoria recognized from her ward work.

"In you go," Lady Agatha directed with a wide sweep of her hand. On the other side was a hallway that looked like it belonged inside a castle. It descended sharply, and flickering lights cast shadows that spoke of a distance to travel.

"After you," Victoria demurred.

Lady Agatha's lips curved in a slight smile. "So, Kathleen taught you a thing or two, did she?"

Victoria looked at her; the approving glimmer in the eye contrasted with a tightening of the hands. The mixed message was troubling. Was Agatha an ally? Or enemy? Or was she simply a teacher?

Uncle Albert came up and tapped his cane lightly in a nullifying pattern on the stone floor as he crossed the threshold into the medieval-looking passage. Many buildings were built atop the older parts of the city. Under the more modern buildings were those that had been buried and abandoned as the city grew up and out over centuries.

"Albert!" Lady Agatha swung to glare at him, her bustle seeming like a weapon as she moved quickly enough that Victoria had to dart away hastily.

Whatever ward had been lingering there, he'd shut it down. That meant it was an unpleasant one. Victoria was impressed. Sometimes Uncle Albert reminded her of the gargoyles: sprinkling small changes and little acts of good here and there—and maybe a few larger ones, like taking her in as his ward. If she still had feelings, she would say she was starting to feel affection for him, so she smiled at him.

"Come, Victoria," Uncle Albert said.

The floor in front of them was thick stone. If she had to guess, she'd say that it had been quarried in one large slab. It was similar to the slick section of stone that was embedded in the great room of her home. She had no idea what it was, but she was sure that it was great for wards. It held even quickly drawn wards longer than most materials, and it took less energy to work them into it.

Despite the descent, Lady Agatha walked with that rat-a-tat rapidity that women adopted in their steps when they were angry and wanted you to know it. She speared Uncle Albert with a look and asked, "Do you have *any* idea how long it took to set that ward?"

He gestured with his walking stick. "This is the main atrium, Victoria. All of the other buildings connect to it. All authorized entrances and exits are through this room. There are no other wards to stop you, but the exits are warded to track who comes and goes."

He paused and met her gaze. Her uncle had already told her that there were ways out of Corvus, but most students didn't find them the first year—or have the ward skills to use the ones they stumbled upon. Victoria wore an athame on her wrist already, but even if she didn't, the lack of a proper athame in hand to draw with wouldn't be an issue for her. Her good riding boots had a small one in the platform, and she still had the corset with an athame in it, too.

"Say goodbye now, Sweeney." Lady Agatha stared at him with narrowed eyes. "You are not, nor will you ever be, faculty at Corvus. Your credentials allow you access to the atrium, and the atrium only."

"I'll be fine, Uncle."

"She'll be in House Invictus," Lady Agatha said. "It connects to the cafeteria and the atrium both."

Uncle Albert met Victoria's eyes, and she nodded. She'd be fine in Invictus. It was just a house. She would have preferred Talhoffer, because combat made more sense to her. Even Ophelia, with the rest of the ward workers, but it didn't matter in the end. The map of the school—which was formed of an entire block of buildings that were connected by passages— was one she'd studied extensively. Uncle Albert had drawn it out as best he recalled, and that information gave her a starting point.

She'd find her way. She was in Glass City, and there were Ravens here she could seek out. After that, she'd find a way to locate Master Nightshade at his country manor so she could speak to him in private. She might have asked to see him again after he'd cured her grief, but she hadn't been thinking clearly at the time.

And sooner or later, she'd meet her cousin, the queen, again.

Victoria was here. That was the first step. After that, she would succeed in her goals, no matter what came next. Eventually, she'd have both answers and vengeance.

CHAPTER 25

◆——◇——◆

CRupert

Rupert perched on the master alchemist's chair and watched him mutter and pace. He waited for the man to notice him. After the fifth circuit of the room, he finally gave up on waiting and coughed.

"Rupes!" Nightshade said.

"You used to be faster to notice me, but you also used to have more hair," Rupert grumbled. It wasn't that he required the hugs that Nightshade used to give him, but he might sometimes miss them more than a little.

"When did you arrive?" Nightshade asked.

Rupert tilted his head. "When the gate opened. Have you become more forgetful?"

"You're funny," Nightshade said cheerily. "Perhaps there is a lot I wish I could forget."

Then the no-longer-child-sized Nightshade embraced him. Rupert shifted from foot to foot when Nightshade petted him atop his head. It felt good to have one of his humans embrace him. Being away from Kat and her children made his stone heart ache.

Silently, as if he'd materialized out of the air itself, Tik revealed himself. "Rupert. Nightshade."

The swordsman did not embrace the gargoyle, but then again, he'd rarely embraced anyone other than Kat.

"Kat," Rupert started. He paused, seeming to have a bit of gravel in his throat, and tried again, "Kat wants Vicky Love to be safe. And you. She wants all of you safe."

"She doesn't want anything now. She's dead," Nightshade snapped.

Rupert stared at him. For a scientist, he could be awfully foolish sometimes. "What Kat *wanted* still exists," Rupert explained. "We need to make sure her wants are honored." He stared at one and then the other. "And find out whatever plan the queen has for Vicky Love, and make sure she and the minor Nightshades and all the rest are safe."

"Minor Nightshades?" Tik said with a slight laugh.

"If he"—Rupert gestured—"is master, they are minor."

Nightshade nodded.

"I altered the potion I gave Victoria," the alchemist said quickly. "She could regain her shadow. It's not easy to do, but it was the best I could manage."

Rupert flew over and patted Nightshade's head—gently so he didn't topple, the way he used to when he was smaller. "This rebellion of yours is a good ripple."

"The queen is not thinking wisely of late," Tik said. "I swore loyalty to the rightful queen after Ev—after *she* changed, and now that Kat is dead . . . my oath is to Victoria, daughter of Kathleen." Tik bowed his head. "I will protect her."

Then he glanced at Nightshade and smiled before adding, "And the minor Nightshades."

Nightshade looked at Rupert and asked, "Did *she* order Kat's death? Or was it the Collective?"

"I do not know," Rupert admitted.

Tik reached out and awkwardly patted Rupert's back. "We'll find out." He paused, squirming in a way that reminded Rupert of the boy he once was instead of the man he'd become. "And don't think . . . I know she's changed, but she loved Kat."

Nightshade sighed. "Love?"

Tik stood taller. "I'm not wrong. I know the queen's different . . ." He shook his head. "But maybe they're *doing* something to her, forcing her somehow."

"Maybe. But Kat is still dead," Rupert said. "And her daughter is in peril."

In silence, the alchemist, the swordsman, and the gargoyle reached out to one another. Family in their way. United to protect the children of their friend and of Nightshade himself.

These humans were not his own young, but sometimes, in moments like these, the old gargoyle thought he'd raised them well all the same.

CHAPTER 26

◆———◆———◆

Milan

The next day, Milan walked into the auditorium for the first meeting of the new students. There were just over sixty kids in the class, and every back row or side row seat was already taken. The only empty seats were the ones in the middle—the ones that left you surrounded on all four sides.

"Must everyone be late?" muttered an austere man at the front of the room. He folded his arms and stared at the students. "I will be your instructor in martial defense—if you are worthy. I am Meister Tik."

"It is now time to start the meeting," said Lady Agatha, sailing into the room like a brightly colored warship. Today, she had an enormous bustle and wore pink flamingo feathers in her hair. "I will be your ward mistress. You may call me Lady Agatha. You've met Mister Tik—"

"Meister," Tik corrected.

Another late student walked into the room. It was Victoria Wardrop, and when she reached the very last row, she smiled at a boy in the end seat. "You are in my chair, so please move."

"There are no assigned seats," the boy replied.

"Correct. However, *that* is my chosen seat."

"Miss Sweeney," Lady Agatha began.

Meister Tik raised a hand to silence her.

"The Corvus Manual clearly states that 'All altercations must allow for an appropriate warning when possible,'" Victoria said to the boy. She spoke quietly, although every person in the room could still hear. "This is your warning."

"Why?"

"Because I *need* to sit in the back." Victoria widened her stance.

From the other side of the room, a girl asked, "Who *are* you?"

"I am *currently* Victoria Sweeney," she said loudly and clearly. "I was once someone different, but my entire family was murdered."

Milan smothered a gasp. He hadn't *known* her parents, had only met her mum that once, but the thought of Lady Wardrop being murdered made his stomach knot.

Victoria reached out and pulled the boy to his feet. "I cannot allow anyone to sit behind me."

Meister Tik threw both hands wide open, as if he would hug her, and stated, "Miss Sweeney will move to my house, and if she can test into it, she can move up to second-year combat to begin."

"Tik! There is a process," Lady Agatha objected. "She's a first-year! You can't simply assign her to Talhoffer *or* to second-year—"

"Bah!" He waved her off. "With her *mother* being who she was, the girl can probably fight as well as you by now."

Milan stared at the teachers and then glanced at Victoria and the boy.

The boy was crawling over unmoving people, who offered him a mix of amusement and pity. Victoria was not watching her failed competitor. She was surveying the rest of the class, as if to identify any threats. She was *nothing* like the girl he'd met that day in the city.

"Seats," boomed the headmaster, entering the room. "It is time to begin. How are we to have a civilized meeting if you are all gawking at . . ." The headmaster looked at Meister Tik and Lady Agatha. "What are they gawking at?"

In low voices, the teachers filled in the new arrival.

Headmaster Edwards lifted his gaze and looked at Victoria. "Miss Sweeney?"

"Headmaster," she greeted him.

"We do not threaten our classmates openly." As he spoke, a tiny blue dragonet crept up his back, gripped one of his ears, and launched itself atop his head.

"You object to my tactics?" Victoria asked.

The headmaster shook his head. "No, child, threats are fine."

The dragonet flapped its wings and hissed in apparent irritation. One drop of saliva fell and set a few of the headmaster's remaining strands of hair on fire.

Absently, the headmaster swatted at his head. "Penelope, mind the hair. That was a good piece I had growing."

The entire student body stared.

Unlike gargoyles, dragonets were rarely glimpsed, although some scientists claimed there were over a thousand in the empire. The guess was based on egg clutch numbers and

156

life expectancy. It probably made sense, but in that moment, all Milan could think was that dragonets shouldn't grin and that the headmaster was as strange as Lady Agatha. Perhaps Master Nightshade wasn't going to be the oddest teacher at Corvus.

"But threats should be delivered subtly," the headmaster told Victoria and the group as a whole.

Duchess Saltwyche—a teacher whose name Milan had caught in low whispers all around—nodded.

What sort of teachers, Milan wondered, suggested that threats or violence against other students was fine? The headmaster might be smiling as if he were a harmless old man, but he was watching Victoria with a creepy sort of interest.

"No," Victoria said loudly. "Subtle threats are only useful if the threat is individual. My *point* was intended for all of these people." She lifted a hand and gestured at the crowd. "It wasn't a threat, Headmaster Edwards. It was a demonstration, to decrease future need for altercations. I cannot allow anyone to sit or stand behind me."

Meister Tik nodded.

The headmaster stared in silence at Victoria for a moment, and then he pronounced, "Penelope says you are meant to be in House Talhoffer."

"Invictus," interjected Lady Agatha. "I took care of it when she arrived. Tik tried to switch her, but—"

A stream of fire shot from between the dragonet's closed teeth toward Lady Agatha, who tossed a ward in front of her quicker than Milan had thought possible.

The headmaster shrugged. "There's no sense in arguing

with Penelope. The girl will be in whichever house the drag-onet says."

Both Lady Agatha and Duchess Saltwyche scowled, but the little dragonet flicked its tail and puffed a plume of smoke with little flickers of flames in it.

Milan wished Victoria had been assigned to his house, but he'd seen how highly the combat master regarded Lady Wardrop. He was relieved that Victoria would be in Meister Tik's house.

The dragonet stared straight at Milan. He forced himself not to look away. He wasn't sure if that was the right thing to do, but he didn't have a better plan.

"What is your name? Who are you?" The words floated into his mind.

Milan gulped and looked around. There was a dragonet talking to him. He tried to think his answer toward the small dragon: "I am Milan. Thief. Student here."

"And thems?" the answer came. The little creature stared at Victoria and then at Algernon.

"Victoria. Algernon. He's a Nightshade."

"Of course. Nights all smell like home." The dragonet hovered above the headmaster briefly. "You smell, too."

Milan glanced at his friend—who was watching Victoria.

That was when he realized that the headmaster was staring at him. He tried to smile, but Headmaster Edwards merely glared.

Milan lowered his head. He had a dragonet—the *head-master's* dragonet—talking to him, and the terrifying girl who had threatened a classmate already was the one he and Algernon were to watch.

Lady Agatha obviously disliked him. Master Nightshade was either mad as a fox or impaired from his potions. And the only other person he knew here was Meredith, who was downright unpleasant.

Honestly, angering the headmaster was just one more thing on a list of troubles.

School was off to a brilliant start.

CHAPTER 27

◆——◇——◆

Algernon

As I was saying," the headmaster continued after another frown toward Milan. "If you were not already assigned a house, you will receive your house assignment and meet your first-year faculty, and we will disperse."

Algernon nodded along with the rest of the students, but he was fixated on the girl from the woods near his house. He *knew* his father and her mother were friends—and that he ought not know that. What he didn't know was why the queen wanted him to watch her.

Maybe his father was being kind, or maybe the queen simply cared about Victoria, since she was the orphan of former Ravens.

Murdered. Her parents and sisters had been murdered. Algernon had never had a mother, but he couldn't imagine losing his father or his brother in such a way. He couldn't believe the girl was at school already.

As she caught him watching her, Victoria stared back at him with flat eyes.

And then the whispers erupted.

"Do you know who *that* is?"

"I'd heard he'd be teaching."

"Didn't he kill that last alchemy teacher?"

Algernon kept his face as blank as he could as his father entered the room. Master Nightshade wandered in, reading something that was clutched in his hand, a letter or a recipe. It was his normal way at home, where Algernon and the other boys moved out of his path. Today, Master Nightshade almost ran into the headmaster and his tiny dragonet.

"Headmaster Edwards, what are you doing in the lab?" Master Nightshade asked, sounding far less alert than he'd done when Algernon had spoken to him lately. Not for the first time, Algernon wondered if it was an act.

"This is the auditorium," Lady Agatha said snippily.

Nightshade looked around. "Excellent. My schedule indicates that I am to attend a meeting at the auditorium now."

Someone snorted as Master Nightshade took a seat.

"This is your alchemy instructor." The headmaster gestured to where Algernon's father sat, looking rumpled, and added, "Master Nightshade did *not* kill the last alchemy teacher."

"Of course I didn't," Master Nightshade said. "Alchemists make medicines and poisons, antidotes and convincers. The only blood I draw is for use in ingredients, and that rarely requires murdering the donor."

Headmaster Edwards did not respond. He looked at the teachers.

"Wards," Lady Agatha said, taking a seat on the far edge of the row of chairs.

"Combat." Tik sat down next to her.

Duchess Saltwyche stood. "Contracts and history."

The headmaster beamed. "We shall be your family as you all embark on your new lives at Corvus."

The teachers were now talking in turns, but Algernon turned his thoughts inward again. *Let them talk.* He'd use the time wisely—to study them and the school.

He'd read the history of the school repeatedly. He'd grown up knowing he'd attend, and in truth, unless he *died*, there was no way to avoid his destiny. Most of the classes he took wouldn't matter: alchemists had little need for combat or manipulation. But the queen had decreed that all of her Ravens had to attend Corvus, and so he was here.

"Young Nightshade!"

When the headmaster said his name, Algernon blinked up at him.

"I thought that was you," the headmaster said in his booming voice. "It's always good to have the next in your line among us. Queen Evangeline will expect updates on you."

The headmaster smiled in a way that told Algernon to be wary. Swamp serpents made him feel the same way.

Algernon saw his father glance at him, but he neither moved nor spoke.

The dragonet flew off the headmaster's shoulder and landed on Algernon's wrist.

"You visit home." The dragonet's words fell into his mind, and Algernon knew without asking that no one else could hear the little dragon. Gargoyles spoke like that, too.

Unsure what to do, Algernon simply stared at it.

"*Her*. Not *it*. I am Pen'lpee." The dragonet stumbled over the name the headmaster had given her.

Algernon smiled. She really was lovely. Without thinking, he lifted his hand to pet her head.

"Careful, young Nightshade," the headmaster said. "Penelope isn't one for strangers touching her."

The dragonet bumped her head against his outstretched fingers.

Obediently, Algernon rubbed the top of her scaled head and down to the edge of her skull. He stopped at the top of her neck. He'd learned last year in the Netherwhere that necks could be ticklish, and tickled dragons sometimes burned people.

"Wouldn't," Penelope muttered.

Algernon continued to pet her head for several moments, forgetting the whispers and the watchers. He missed the Netherwhere when he was away from it too long. A few times, he'd even left an ingredient off a list in order to go back more than he strictly *needed* to go.

"Can go from here." Penelope looked at him, staring directly into his eyes. "Pen'lpee show you. Don't tell. Master 'Dward say no going."

Then the little dragonet flew away and landed on the headmaster's now outstretched arm.

"Penelope seems to like you." Headmaster Edwards frowned.

Algernon met the headmaster's gaze and lied. "Sorry. There was a dragonet that came by Nightshade Manor a few times. I guess I missed seeing her."

"Hmm. Welcome to Corvus, Young Nightshade. May you soon succeed at your tasks."

Algernon tensed. It was, on the surface, a harmless thing to wish someone well, but *his* tasks included learning enough to eventually murder his own father.

Algernon hoped his father had the sense to be cautious—and that he could figure out how to get close to Victoria. And, well, figure out how to manage classes, navigate the school, and not revert to stuttering if a girl—even Meredith—spoke to him. He wished he were home, wished he weren't a Nightshade, and suddenly wanted to run away to the Netherwhere.

But wishes weren't going to help.

As the students were dismissed, Algernon lost track of Milan in the sea of students, but when he turned to look for him, it was not the thief but the girl who stood at his side.

"I met your father before this," Victoria said abruptly. "He cured me of grief."

Algernon was shocked out of his awkwardness. "That's not possible."

"Are you suggesting that I'm *wrong*?"

"I saw you before. With your family," Algernon said, ignoring her question. He remembered how happy she'd been, and he hurt for her. "I'm sorry about them."

"Did you kill them?"

"No! I would never—"

"Then don't be sorry," she said coldly. "The people who did it *will* be sorry. It's why . . ." Her voice faltered, and she sounded less chilly for a moment, but then she took a steadying breath. "It's why I'm here."

Victoria stopped talking and scowled. Algernon had the urge to help her. He wasn't sure how or with what, but he remembered her family. He announced, "We're going to be friends now."

"What?" Her eyes widened as if he had just belched in her face.

"I'm Algernon. I'll be your friend. That means you'll probably need to get to know Milan, too. He's my . . . cousin."

Victoria folded her arms. "You said I was *wrong*. Why?"

Algernon stepped closer to Victoria and said, "My father is not able to cure grief. Do you mean he gave you calmers?"

"Before he cured me, yes." She gestured at the ground where the wall lights weren't casting a shadow. "He took my shadow."

"It's dark in here." Algernon was mystified, though. She *had* to be wrong, but if anyone could break the laws of science, it was his father.

Victoria waited until every other student had left the room, and then she said, "You don't have cousins. There are no other Nightshades. You and the spare. That's all."

"Milan lived at the manor, and he's here with me. He's the same as a cousin. We are *both* your friends now."

"You can't simply *declare* friendship," Victoria objected. "There is a whole process."

"What is it?"

Victoria's jaw was clenched so tightly that he was certain it had to hurt her. She studied him, much as the dragonet had done earlier, and then—as if she were reading the words—said, "Friends are those with common interests, shared experiences, and mutual goals. They trust as a result of this, and they demonstrate loyalty."

As she was speaking, Milan joined them.

Victoria stepped back slightly.

"I am interested in being your friend," Algernon announced. He held up one finger. "Mutual goals."

"That's not mutual," Milan objected. He nodded at Victoria in greeting. "Vicky, I'm sorry to hear about your mother and family."

"Victoria," she corrected.

Algernon got her attention again. "We are *mutually not interested* in succeeding here."

Victoria paused and then nodded. "Fine."

"And you can trust me," he added quickly. "Us."

But Victoria simply shook her head and walked away, leaving him standing in the hallway with Milan.

"Be careful." Milan folded his arms.

"Do you know her?"

Milan shook his head. "I saw her and her mum in the city once."

Algernon knew enough about thieves to realize that there was more to the story than what Milan said.

What Milan *did* say was, "Do dragonets talk to a lot of people?"

"No," Algernon said quietly. "They do not."

"The headmaster looked unhappy about it."

"True." Algernon paused, grinned, and added, "Well, we're off to a grand start at not succeeding!"

Milan did not look amused at all, and Algernon knew he ought not find it funny either. But laughing had made things in the Netherwhere easier. It had made things at Nightshade Manor easier, too. And if they could face toxic smoke and dangerous creatures, surely a few teachers were manageable.

CHAPTER 28

◆——————◇——————◆

Victoria

Victoria spent hours walking around the school. Corvus was a series of connecting buildings, and from the outside, it was impossible to gauge the size of the school. The main building, where she had once stopped with her mother, was drab. The other facades that were visible from the street, Victoria now realized, appeared like homes. Each faculty member apparently entered a different door, but their quarters all connected to the school.

To Victoria's mind, that meant that there were many doors *out* that she could find—if she was willing to break into a faculty home. She filed that detail away as she traveled the passages and staircases of the school.

Unexpectedly, Victoria turned a corner and was hit with a spider-silk ward. She found herself wrapped in sticky strands of web that pinned her to the stone wall.

"Wardrop." Meredith, the girl from the Glass Castle, stood there with an athame in her hand. "I was hoping we could meet."

"Release me."

Meredith came closer. She was just as pretty as she'd been at court, even in common clothes. "You embarrassed me," Meredith said. "You humiliated me at *court*."

Embarrassed? Victoria hadn't intended to do that, and embarrassment wasn't anywhere on the list of things Victoria had time to consider, even when she'd had emotions. She glared at the girl and concentrated on slipping a small thin knife from where it was hidden on the underside of her forearm.

"The queen," Meredith continued. "We were before the queen, and—"

"*I* was before the queen," Victoria corrected her. "You were just . . . there."

Meredith poked the web cocoon that trapped Victoria. "You stay out of my way." She poked again. "And away from the palace."

"I was *summoned* there," Victoria pointed out. She didn't escape the web yet. She wasn't in fatal danger, so revealing the extent of her ward skills seemed unnecessary.

A group of students appeared from the direction Victoria had been headed.

"Merry?" One of the boys scurried toward them. "Do you know who she *is*?"

Meredith smiled in a very convincing way. She stepped back until she was against the opposite wall and added, "Of course! We met at court."

At that point, Victoria had worked the knife into her hand and sliced open the cocoon. She landed half crouched with a thump and stood quickly.

Calmly, she threw her knife toward the wall where Meredith was now standing, intentionally grazing the edge of the girl's hair. It was warning enough.

"Missed," one of the boys said.

Victoria walked over and pulled the knife out, releasing the ringlet that she'd stuck to the wall. "What do you think, *Merry*? Did I miss?"

The older girl's smile slipped toward a scowl.

"Merry," one of the other kids said in warning.

Victoria felt multiple gazes on her back as she stepped around the group and continued on her way. She had no interest in petty enemies. Just as she had no interest in friends. What she needed was skills, lessons, secrets explained, and her new sword . . .

A few minutes later, she entered through a thick door into her new dormitory. The middle of the first room had no furniture. There was a line in the floor, marked by a different color of stone, that formed a giant rectangle for sparring.

Victoria continued into the dormitory until she found her bedroom—and her roommates. Both girls were there as if they had been waiting for her. She walked into the room warily, pulling energy into her athame, just in case there was a challenge. A combat dorm might have such a tradition.

"Wards and combat?" the first girl asked astutely. She was sitting on her bed with a book in hand and a dagger at her knee.

"Yes," Victoria said cautiously.

"I'm Nora. Third-year." She gestured to the other girl. "And . . ."

"Ida. Second-year." Ida didn't get out of bed. She rolled to her side and propped her head up on her hand. She was pretty, but her pale-red hair would make her too memorable for some of a Raven's tasks.

"You're a firstie . . . but that wasn't a basic ward surge."

Victoria shrugged.

"We are your allies here," Nora said. "Very few girls sort into combat. *None* do first year. There's us and two others. We can all choose to start over in a new house after our first year—"

"I didn't choose anything," Victoria interrupted, standing awkwardly near the door. "I inherited it."

Nora nodded. "The Wardrops were an asset to the empire. I extend my sympathy for your loss."

Ida nodded and said softly, "You're safe here with us."

Victoria made a disbelieving noise. "Nowhere is safe," she said firmly.

Then she walked past their beds to hers. As the youngest, her bed was closest to the wall. In theory, that was the safest position in the room. Doors were easier to enter than windows, so proximity to the window was safer than to the door. Such thoughts were sword-and-dagger thoughts. Wards meant that walls could be as easy to break as doors.

But in the ward workers' dorms, she suspected the security was not as likely to account for bladed weapons. Mama had once explained that people think from only the boots they wear, but the Wardrops wore many types of boots. Doing both wards and weapons changed how the world looked.

As she scanned the area around her bed, Victoria discovered a sealed envelope resting on her trunk. She reached out, touching her athame to the edge of it in search of wards. The only one present was a fingerprint ward—which meant that no one else could read the contents of the envelope. She broke the seal and withdrew a folded sheet of paper.

Miss Sweeney,

Female students in Talhoffer are rare. You are one of only five girls in all of House Talhoffer. As such, it has become tradition that each young lady may take two beds, one for weapons and one for sleeping or, if preferred, two for sleeping.

Welcome to my house. I shall expect you at the combat rooms directly after breaking your fast the day after tomorrow.

I was deeply saddened to learn of your loss. Your mother was one of the finest fighters I've known and a treasured friend.

Meister Tik
House Talhoffer
Corvus Combat Master

Victoria read it a second time, and then she folded the page and drew a simple fire ward to incinerate the letter. Her roommates had turned away to give her privacy as she got settled, but Nora glanced her way as she burned the note.

Once the letter was reduced to ashes, Victoria walked to the end of the row of beds and pushed two beds together so her weapons were in easy reach.

As settled as she could be, Victoria gathered several of her schoolbooks, a notebook, pen, and ink and crawled into her bed to study.

If she had still been able to feel loneliness, she suspected that she'd feel it now.

CHAPTER 29

Victoria

Morning came quickly. Since losing her shadow, Victoria had discovered that she needed very little sleep. She dressed, feeling the zing of the second athame touching her skin when she laced her corset. This particular corset was designed so she didn't need assistance lacing it. The final jolt when she slipped her feet into her boots was always enough that she had to pause and think about releasing the accumulated energy that three athames drew.

It wasn't a choice.

Every athame pulled a slight amount of energy when it touched a ward worker's skin. Victoria instinctively pulled more energy every time, which meant that the reservoir she held in case she needed it was on the wrong side of comfortable. But it also meant she was primed for defensive wards at all times.

She'd tried *offensive* wards, but at the back of her mind, Victoria could always hear her mother's voice. Her defensive wards, however, were strong. Attempting to touch her when she was well warded would result in the sort of electric shock that dropped most people.

One of her two new roommates, Ida, was awake and watching her.

"Let's get breakfast," Ida suggested.

"I like silence," Victoria announced abruptly. "You *may* join me for breakfast, but only if you don't speak."

Ida stared at her for a moment and then burst into giggles. It was odd.

Victoria frowned and began lacing her boots.

"I'll meet you in the dining hall," Ida said, leaving Victoria alone with her thoughts.

Little acts of good, she reminded herself. Being kind to Ida was good. It was a ripple, according to the gargoyles, of good in the world. She had no idea if they were right, but for now, it would be her guiding rule because it seemed like how her parents had acted—and how they'd wanted her to be.

As she walked alone to the dining hall, Victoria saw only two or three students, but the sun wasn't yet up. And most of the older students weren't even arriving until today.

Inside the hall, the tables ranged from two-person square tables to rectangular tables that would seat up to ten. The room had high ceilings with skylights, several of which were always open so gargoyles could fly in and out—many of the creatures were perched on the beams that stretched across the open space.

As Victoria placed her tray of oatmeal and bread on a table, she looked up and saw Kingly.

"Ward girl," he said in greeting.

She smiled, feeling the first rush of emotions she'd experienced since she'd had her shadow severed. She was *happy* to see the gargoyle—which frightened her. She wasn't supposed to have any emotions since her cure, and she wondered if it was the gargoyle's magic. She frowned at him and said, "I feel things, but . . . I shouldn't."

"You should feel," Kingly said in her mind. His words felt heavier than she remembered.

"I don't ever want—"

"But you will," Kingly said, and then he turned away, leaving Victoria sitting there. She was still sitting when Milan and Algernon arrived.

Milan wandered off to get food, and Algernon pulled out the chair opposite her but didn't sit.

"You haven't had any etiquette classes, have you?" Victoria asked.

"I'm going to live at Nightshade Manor and concoct poisons that people like you will deliver," he said bluntly. "Why do I need etiquette?"

"What if you don't want to be an alchemist?"

"Then I'll be killed, and my brother will be stuck doing it."

"Sit." Victoria nodded toward the chair.

Algernon grinned at her and sat. "I miss my brother. Alistair and I grew up mostly just us, but my father started bringing home orphans—boys, so they're almost like brothers. They come and go, except Milan."

Victoria sighed, ripped a piece of bread from the chunk she

had beside her bowl, and ate it. "I suppose sharing stories is another way to make us friends, then?"

Algernon smiled.

Milan was already headed toward them, as was Ida. Both had trays of food.

"A friend of yours?" Ida asked.

"No," Victoria answered.

"Yes," Algernon said at the exact same moment.

Ida laughed.

Algernon said, "Victoria is a little temperamental."

"Same house, poppet. I'm aware of who she is." Ida offered him a curtsy that appeared to somehow be a joke and glanced at Milan. "And you?"

"His cousin," Milan said.

"Not a bad liar." Ida looked at them with a smug expression. "You"—she pointed at Algernon—"would be the next in line to be the Queen's Alchemist. A something or other, as with all the Nightshades."

She turned to Milan as if to jab his shoulder. "That makes you one of the thieves his father collects."

Milan caught her wrist.

She twisted free of Milan's hand and kicked his knee out.

Milan stumbled but caught himself before falling.

"Violence must always have a *reason*, Ida, else it's brutish." Victoria stood and stepped between her and the boys. "There is a treatise by Howard the Hairless on this topic."

Ida nodded. "But Ethel of the Wild Highland Plains countered that in *Argument Moste Foule*, in which *she* noted that establishing one's ferocity sometimes requires initial brute-like acts. I believe you demonstrated much the same at the initial assembly."

Victoria looked at Ida, and then at Milan's knee, and then around the room, where she saw other students watching their small group. "Valid."

Milan glanced at Algernon and said, "It's possible that Meredith is the *least* frightening girl here."

"Meredith?" Victoria echoed.

"She's a girl in our house. Alchemist," Algernon explained.

"Meredith is in the alchemy house?" Victoria asked. "But she's a ward worker."

Milan shrugged.

"I would like to know more about her," Victoria said. "We had an encounter."

"Really?" Algernon looked alarmed.

"Yes. She tried to pin me to a wall."

"We can find out why," Milan offered.

"There is no mystery: she dislikes me." Victoria shook her head. Without emotions, everything seemed clearer.

Algernon announced, "I won't be her friend. If she thinks she can threaten you—"

"Fine." Victoria got up and walked away.

Ida, however, kept pace with her.

"Told you they were your friends," Ida added with a smug smile as they walked toward their classes.

When Victoria grimaced, Ida offered a new word. "How about *allies*? Everyone needs those."

Allies.

That sounded all right to her—friends without emotions. Victoria didn't want to jeopardize her emotion-free state. She could not imagine risking *caring*, like one did for a friend. Caring led to pain, and she was never going to endure that again.

"Fine," Victoria agreed. "We can be allies."

CHAPTER 30

◆———◆———◆

Victoria

Everyone did, indeed, need allies. Victoria knew that. Even her mother had allies. Master Nightshade. Marta the blacksmith. Meister Tik.

Victoria was planning to retrieve her sword from Marta's shop, now that she was in Glass City.

She approached Ida.

"Since we are allies," she told her, "you may assist me on a mission tonight."

Ida burst into laughter. "You are funny, Victoria Wardrop. I'm *glad* we're allies."

"You are?"

"Sure," said Ida. "You want to break out of school and go on a mission. Probably dangerous..." She glanced at Victoria, who nodded. "You are exactly the sort of friend I was hoping to make."

LATER THAT NIGHT, Victoria dressed carefully for their outing. She covered her attire with a thick cloak that Uncle

Albert had provided. It was a heavy, dark leather, resistant to most stains and lined for warmth. Most importantly, a breeze wouldn't stir it and reveal the small sword she hid at her side.

"Do you know how to get out?" Ida asked.

They were already behind a silencing ward as Victoria selected a few tools to carry with them. "Do you have a weapon with you?"

Ida gave her a look before hiking up her skirts to show a long, thin blade strapped to one leg and an overlong dagger on the other.

Ida dropped her skirts and said, "I've been armed most of my life."

"Me too." Victoria nodded. Admittedly, her typical weaponry had been an athame.

"The alchemist won't be armed," she told Ida, half expecting inquiries on why she was bringing him. "And I don't know if the thief is coming."

Ida shrugged. "Don't need them, do we?"

They slipped out of the bedroom and skirted around various wards in the hallways. Victoria disabled several of them as she passed. Who left a *blisters* ward randomly out where first-year students could get caught in it?

When they reached the hallway where the House Valentinus dorms were, Ida gestured upward. "Step back," she said. "Liquid fire."

Victoria wasn't sure she could disable it safely with a ward. It would be foolish to make a door so accessible, but alchemists were capable of slipping a poison to you for punishment.

As Victoria kept debating how to disable it, Ida reached out and . . . *knocked*.

A few moments passed, and the door opened.

"We are here to see Nightshade," Ida announced.

A boy opened his mouth to speak, but when he saw Victoria, he blurted out, "Stay here, *please*. I'll tell him."

The door closed as quickly as the boy could manage it. Ida glanced at Victoria. Then she clamped a hand over her mouth, making her laughter sound vaguely like snorts and gulps.

"What? Why is this amusing?"

"They're all acting as if you are terrifying."

"Why aren't *you* afraid of me?" Victoria asked.

Ida shrugged. "You seem logical. If people act logically around you, they'll be fine. I find you very comforting, to be honest."

They both looked toward the door as it opened again.

Algernon was alone.

"I'm going to Steel Close," Victoria announced. "You may stay or come."

Ida whistled low.

"What's that?" Algernon asked.

"Weapons Alley," Ida clarified. "Most people don't go there alone, and there's a fair chance of a fight."

Algernon took a deep breath and said, "I'm not a fighter. Why do you want me to come, Victoria?"

"In books, friends either go on the missions, or later they will need to be rescued. I used to read a lot before . . . before, when I lived with my family. I don't want to have to rescue you."

"All right, then," Algernon said, "Lead the way."

At the atrium, Victoria drew a nullifying ward to remove the same ward that Uncle Albert had removed upon their arrival. "Hand each on my shoulder."

Ida and Algernon touched her shoulders, and she quickly sketched a defensive ward that would make them impossible to see as they walked out the front door.

They were a half block from Corvus when she dropped the ward.

"Well, *that's* not first-year ward work," Ida said. "It's not even something they cover in the fourth year!"

Victoria shrugged and scanned the streets as they walked. A few thieves were out and about, and neither Algernon nor Ida seemed as alert as she would have liked them to be. She wished Milan had joined them.

"Turn here. *Now.*"

They obeyed, swerving into a shadowed alley.

"Too many watchers out there," she explained, slipping her small sword from under her cloak.

Algernon drew a sharp breath, and then another when Ida drew a short blade from under her skirt.

"If we stay along the edge of the canal, we can avoid most people." Victoria pointed toward the dark water with her sword and then started walking again. "Watch the water, though. Kelpies are fast, and we need to be alert to dodge them."

Algernon smiled. "I'm used to kelpies."

Victoria raised her brows as they moved through the puddle-filled edge of the road—toward where Steel Close and her new swords were waiting. She'd never heard anyone sound so relaxed about *kelpies*, of all things.

Later she would need to ask Algernon a few questions.

CHAPTER 31

◆——◇——◆

Milan

M ilan slipped out of bed and made his way to the door.
He'd told Algernon he wasn't feeling well, because he
wanted to go on a trip of his own to visit some old acquain-
tances on the street. If anyone had heard something about
Victoria's mother, it would be Florie.

"Escaping?"

Milan glanced upward and found the owner of the voice
curled up in a window casement. Meredith was a good eight
feet up, tucked in where few would look.

"Nightshade Junior left with a couple Talhoffers earlier."

Meredith's foot dangled down, and Milan glimpsed what
looked like an athame on her leg. However, it was wickedly
curved and it glinted like it was more dagger than device.
"Weapon or ward tool?"

She lifted one shoulder in a half shrug. "Depends on the
problem. It's a tool either way, just sometimes I need the
pointy part and sometimes I need the magic."

"Why not carry two?"

"Who says I don't?" Meredith hopped down, landing in the hall in a crouch—like a thief would. Her one hand touched the ground briefly before she stood.

"You're street-born?"

"I was in Moscow's house," she said softly.

Milan frowned. Meredith was a series of contradictions. She worked wards, but she was in the Corvus group for alchemy. She'd insisted on formal manners when he and Algernon met her, but she was from the same streets where Milan had worked.

Meredith started walking, and Milan kept pace.

"Everyone says Moscow was cruel," he said.

She didn't reply for a bit, choosing instead to absently draw silencing wards and drop them. Finally, she said, "Yes."

She obviously didn't want to say more, so he didn't ask. All he said was, "I was with Florie."

She nodded. "He's fair."

And that was all there was to say about that.

As they walked, a dragonet flew around them, chasing what appeared to be a group of three faeries. There was something comforting to Milan about the way the Netherwhere creatures coexisted at Corvus.

"Are you going to go see Florie?" she asked suddenly.

"I was looking for a door."

Meredith nodded to a high casement. "I have a door."

As he studied the rock wall around it, he could see places where the wall jutted out or dipped inward.

Meredith pulled a series of straps on her skirt, causing it to hitch up in various places. Under it, she wore the pantaloons he'd seen other female thieves wear.

Wall climbing *and* a trip out with a fellow thief? He followed without pause. It wasn't about seeing Florie anymore. It was about remembering who he was—and figuring out who Meredith *really* was.

Outside the school, Milan breathed easier. His thief mannerisms made him feel anxious inside the school.

"How do you do it?" He gestured to Corvus and then to the city.

She shrugged. "I survive. Same as on the streets."

They walked for a few more minutes, and he was starting to wonder if Meredith had a destination in mind. Then she smiled the sort of smile that every thief gets when they're about to try something dangerous. "How bold are you feeling?"

Milan looked around until he saw what she was eyeing. A gold-and-scarlet royal carriage was parked near the theater.

"No."

"If you can get *one* royal trinket, I'll . . . What do you want? Name your terms," Meredith said. "If *I* get one, I want your trust."

He shook his head. "You can't win trust in a bet."

"Fine. One free pass," she said.

"Not if whatever you're doing endangers Algernon or Victoria."

Meredith pressed her lips together. "Done. What do you want?"

"The same thing. A pass—to do or to stop doing something."

"Agreed."

187

Thieves could change appearances between one step and the next, but Meredith seemed like an illusionist. She walked taller, and her steps grew closer. Her shoulders were steady and set, and her chin tilted as if she were royalty herself.

The curtain in window of the carriage fluttered, and Milan stalked off after her.

"Arm," she ordered.

He frowned but did as he was told. Meredith's hand rested on his arm, much the way a gargoyle's talon-tipped feet curled over a ledge. He glanced upward at the gargoyles above him watching—and promptly stumbled when he heard one say, "Steady on, boy-thing."

Milan felt silly, but it was no wonder he tripped. A gargoyle had never spoken to him. He stared at it.

"Be brave," it said.

The door of the carriage opened, and there she was! The Glass Queen herself.

Queen Evangeline looked at them. "And what are *you* doing at my carriage door?"

Meredith curtsied and somehow managed to pull Milan into a bow in the same move.

"Planning to rob you, Your Majesty," Meredith pronounced.

Milan gulped. He wanted to lie, to say something, anything. He wasn't sure what the punishment was for stealing from the queen, but he didn't want to find out.

"*Meredith*, tell her you were joking," he demanded.

"Oh pish, the queen knows I try to lift something from her pockets every time I see her." Meredith flashed a half quirk of a smile. "It's how I ended up at Corvus."

"Meredith tried to relieve me of a lovely bracelet when I first met her," Queen Evangeline said.

Milan stared at Meredith. "You tried to *steal the queen's bracelet*?"

Meredith laughed. "I *did* steal it, but one of the Ravens caught me."

"And when you become a Raven, it's yours, dear. I've given my word." The queen leaned back in her seat and looked down at them.

The queen then turned her full attention to Milan. "Who are you, then?"

"Milan . . . Your Majesty." He bobbed his head again in another bow.

"And you are hoping to be one of my Ravens, too," the Glass Queen said. "Meredith is well on her way to a bright future. You are wise to befriend her."

Milan squirmed. "We aren't—"

"I see," the queen interrupted. "You're one of Aloysius's orphans, I believe. Milan, is it? The name you said. Are you the one who upset Horatio?"

"Who?"

"Headmaster Edwards," Meredith said.

"I hear you just showed up at Corvus without an invitation. Alongside the Nightshade heir."

"I guess," Milan said. It hadn't occurred to him that he wasn't welcome. Master Nightshade had brought him, and Milan had assumed he'd had permission. He was about to go on when he caught Meredith's triumphant look.

One of the shining red jewels from the queen's cloak was

missing. She'd managed to secure something to win their bet. He'd been so overwhelmed by the queen's speaking to him that he'd all but forgotten.

"There will be a reception during the winter holidays," the queen said. "I will expect you both at court with news from the underground." Then Queen Evangeline motioned for the guard, who had remained silent the entire time. "And, Meredith?"

"Yes, Your Majesty?"

"Don't take a second of those from my cloak, child." The queen smiled in amusement. "Your companion exposed you when he looked at the spot from which you've stolen another of my things."

Meredith widened her eyes. "Oh my! There is a gem missing. Are those rubies?"

"Garnets," the queen said. "Would you happen to have one?"

"Perhaps it tore when you entered the carriage?" Meredith looked at the ground as if she were searching for a fallen gemstone.

The queen laughed. "I didn't see you do it, nor did Alaric, I assume?" She glanced at her guard, who frowned but shook his head.

"You do please me, Meredith," the queen said with a satisfied smile. She lifted her gaze to meet Milan's eyes. "If she steals without my noticing, she can keep her treasure. She is *not* permitted to relieve my guests of more than five total trinkets at any given event."

Milan's mouth opened soundlessly again.

"You caught her. You should be compensated for that." The

queen reached down to her cloak and pulled a stone free with a tug. She tossed it toward him.

Milan snatched it from the air.

"Being *my* Raven is not without its benefits," the queen pronounced. "Remember that. And tell Nightshade that I think you'll make a fine Raven. Show him that"—she nodded—"but do not give it away."

Then the door closed, and Milan was left standing in the dark with Meredith. They watched in silence as the carriage rolled away. The cab swayed gently on the uneven streets.

Milan whispered, "I just met the queen."

As he looked upward, the gargoyle that had spoken earlier was still there, staring back at him. "Steady, boy-beast. Ask questions. Stay steady. The girl needs you."

Milan gave a quick dip of his eyes rather than nodding. He wasn't sure whether "the girl" was Victoria or Meredith, or even the queen herself. Gargoyles, he knew, took a different view of time and age.

"I need to meet Florie," Meredith said. "The queen wants news."

CHAPTER 32

◆ ◇ ◆

Algernon

Algernon followed Victoria with a sort of mix of fear and awe. He missed the Netherwhere and the creatures there, so watching the canal for kelpies was making him grin, even when a man stepped out of the mouth of a close that was signed as B ood C ose. Algernon stared at the sign again.

"Blood Close," he read as he saw that the missing letters were actually there, but drawn in something dark and red.

The man drew a sword, and the shivery sound of metal sliding free of its scabbard made Algernon flinch.

"You need to come with me, girl," the man said, staring at Victoria.

Ida stepped closer to Algernon, giving Victoria more space to fight.

Victoria was quick. Her strikes were too fast for Algernon to follow, but he could tell neither fighter was winning.

"Should you help?" Algernon asked Ida as quietly as he could.

Ida gave him the sort of look his father gave failed experiments, but he had no idea how sword fights worked. He'd never seen a real one until today.

As if a fight weren't trouble enough, Algernon saw a herd of kelpies racing toward shore, hooves churning a white foam so the sea frothed like smoke.

"Ida?"

She followed his gaze. As soon as she saw the kelpies, Ida stepped in front of Algernon and raised her sword.

A kelpie leaped from the water. But instead of attacking them, the kelpie grabbed the man Victoria was fighting.

"Victoria!" Algernon yelled.

A gargoyle flew in with a loud thrum of wings. It stood in front of Victoria—just like Ida was standing in from Algernon.

The man scrambled to escape the kelpie biting his leg. His sword cut through Ida's skirt and sliced through her boot.

Then a massive woman with goggles in one hand and a longsword in the other stalked toward them.

"Well, go on, then," the woman said.

A kelpie craned its massive head and neck forward, clamped down on the man's other ankle and dragged him into the sea.

Ida pushed to her feet, obviously injured to some degree.

They were still in the dark, facing a woman with a sword and kelpies at her command.

"Thank you, Uncle Millicent," Victoria said softly as the gargoyle left. For a moment, her voice sounded gentle, and her smile made her look like the girl he'd seen in the woods near Nightshade Manor.

"What are you doing down here at this hour, girl?"

"Hello, Miss Marta," Victoria said. "I . . . didn't know how else to reach you. I'd like to collect my birthday gift."

The woman let out a loud sigh. "Come on, then." Miss Marta nodded to Ida. "No need to hide her injury. We'll get her fixed up at the shop." She gestured with her sword. "It's right up the way."

By the time they reached the shop, Ida was visibly wincing.

"Let's see," Marta ordered.

Ida yanked her boot off and tugged up the bottom of her skirt, only as high as the knee. "Just a scratch," Ida said. "Stings, though."

At that, Algernon walked over and sniffed the cut.

"His blade had a blood-thinning tincture on it." He pointed. "See the tooth-looking red lines? That's from a potion with serpent venom. You'll bleed out."

Victoria muttered a word that Algernon pretended not to hear.

"I need salt water," Algernon started.

"And iron," Marta finished. "Not the first poisoned blade I've met."

She pointed to a giant cupboard. "Third shelf, Vicky. Brown bottle with a stopper and a red label." Then she grabbed a bucket and walked to the edge of her shop where there was no wall. Calmly, as though the sea weren't filled with kelpies, merrows, and serpents, she bent and pulled a bucket of water out of the sea.

When she brought it and a stained white cloth over, Algernon looked at it to make sure it was serpent-free.

"This will hurt," he warned Ida as he dipped the cloth in the water.

After he pressed the salt water to her ankle, Ida snatched the cloth and said, "I'll do it myself."

He watched her clean the poisons until the red lines were faded to nothing more than thin white lines. Then he took the jar of iron that Victoria was still holding and started layering on the thick iron shavings.

"I'm sorry about Kat and Wilbur," Marta said in a low voice as she pulled down a long package that clearly held swords.

"Thank you." Victoria unwrapped the swords and lifted one. Maybe it was the way she held it, or maybe it was the way the light reflected wrongly from its surface, but it was obvious that there was something special about this sword.

"Your parents wouldn't want you looking for trouble, Vicky."

"They're dead." Victoria held the sword upright in front of her. "I'm going after whoever did it."

"You can trust Tik." Marta glanced at him. "The Nightshades, too."

Victoria lowered the blade. "And my cousin?"

"I wish I knew," Marta said. "She has the match to your blade. Worried about her safety."

Algernon frowned. Cousin? The Wardrops had no family he knew of. Was Victoria in danger still? He'd have to ask his father if the crown knew who had killed her family. From the way Victoria and Miss Marta were acting, they didn't think the threat had ended.

Marta hugged Victoria with one arm, and then she escorted all three of them back to Corvus and left them at the front door.

CHAPTER 33

✦ ◇ ✦

Meredith

Walking through Glass City with a fellow thief was comfortable. Milan was like her—a thief who understood the street—but he was also trusted by Nightshade and obviously loyal to the Wardrop girl.

"Have you met Florie before?" Milan asked as he led Meredith through an alley.

"No. Moscow wasn't social with other houses," she said.

"Right," Milan said. "I heard Moscow was sent on a resettlement ship. They said he beat a kid near to death."

Merry felt her heartbeat increase, but she'd learned—from Moscow, in fact—to keep fear out of her voice most of the time.

"Yes. I'm glad someone turned him in," she said, but she didn't add that *she* was that someone.

Milan led her to an old stone door that was visible only after pushing through a waterfall of vines. He knocked. Six times. Paused. Three times more. After a moment, the door creaked open, but only far enough for Milan to reach inside and show the scar from when he'd joined Florie's house.

All thieves had a scar from a burn that was applied by the house coin.

"Milan?" a voice asked as the door slid open further.

"And a fr—a *guest*," he added, not looking at Meredith.

They went inside, then down several staircases and onto a cobblestone road. This was part of the city *under* the city. As water levels had risen, the city was built atop the last century's buildings. Now the streets and buildings that were once on the street level had become an underground warren of places and passages that the thieves had claimed to make their home. It flooded sometimes, but there were still plenty of places dry enough for the city's lost children.

"You brought a nob?" a boy with corkscrew curls asked Milan.

"She's one of us, Rott."

It wasn't a homecoming like in paintings, but a few thieves made their way to greet Milan and stare at Meredith. He was liked, and because of it, she was welcomed.

"Who's this?" Florie said as he rolled over to join them. He was only eighteen, younger than most thieves with their own houses, but he was terrifying enough to protect his family of criminals.

He sat in a slightly lopsided chair with enormous wheels. It served as both a towering throne and as a medical assistance chair. In it, he could roll over obstacles—and cobblestones.

"Classmate from Corvus." Milan stared up at Florie as if he was expecting a rebuke.

"I'm glad you're going to school." Florie sounded proud.

"But why'd you bring *her*? Nobs got no business in the underground."

Meredith pushed her sleeve up and unsealed the ward that hid her house scar. The ugliness made it clear that she'd resisted. "Not a nob."

Florie met her eyes. "Moscow was a brute."

"May the maggots eat well," she murmured.

Florie laughed before pivoting in his chair and rolling away, vanishing into his underground kingdom. Milan followed Florie, and Meredith trailed behind him as they descended deeper into the labyrinth of passages.

"I have heard of you, Merry Moscow." Florie's voice echoed back as he steered his chair down small ramp that had been cut in the floor.

"You're . . . *Merry Moscow*?" Milan asked.

She shrugged. Thieves didn't have surnames, typically. Florie's people used only a city name, no surnames. Some houses used flowers or herbs. There was always a clue to identify house affiliation, but the thieves in Moscow's house all had to add *his* name as part of theirs. Merry hated him extra for it. She was her own person, not property.

"I've heard of you," Milan said quietly.

She flashed him a smile. "The crown jewelry job or the nob hill one?"

"Both," Milan murmured in what sounded like awe.

She couldn't blame him. The tower where the jewels were often stored was the second-highest building in the city.

Florie stopped in what had once been a courtyard. Thieves

appeared out of the shadows with a table. They plopped it in front of Florie. Two chairs, for Milan and Merry, appeared next. Food was brought in: fruits that were only a day or two past selling time, chunks of cheese, nearly fresh bread, and a pot of savory stew.

"I'm just *Merry* now," she told Florie and Milan both. "Someday I'll be Lady Meredith. The queen will give me a surname of my own when I become a Raven."

"She already knows the queen," Milan said, and Merry liked the awe in his voice.

Merry handed Florie the garnet she stole. "The queen sent me to Corvus."

"The palace doesn't often care for thieves." Florie put the garnet on the table next to him as he scooped stew into a large chunk of bread, creating an edible bowl. "A special few who make Ravens, maybe, but not those of us on the streets."

Merry squared her shoulder and announced, "It will when *I* am her advisor. Do you think it was an accident that Moscow was sent away? That others haven't been? I'm making changes *already*."

No one laughed. They listened. And that made Merry feel warmer than even the good meal and warm boots she'd earned by entering Corvus.

Florie said, "It is good to have allies, Lady Meredith. Most of us don't end up guarding the queen." He glanced at Milan. "Or confidant to her chief poisoner."

Milan shrugged like he was embarrassed, but Merry knew that Florie was as clever as people said and that he was protective of his people. Every ally mattered, but the *right* allies mattered more. One day, she hoped to change the world for the people society had cast aside.

"What do you hear about the Wardrops?" Merry asked quietly, finally getting to the heart of why she was here.

Florie folded his hands and met her eyes. "Who asks? The Collective? The queen? Nightshade?"

He glanced at Milan. Thieves were always underestimated, but they were the eyes of the city—and Lady Wardrop had been one of their own before she was a Raven.

"The queen," Merrie said.

Florie nodded. "Word down deep and low is that the people who wanted Lady Wardrop gone want the queen gone, too."

Merry sighed. "The Collective, then?"

Florie shrugged. "Perhaps, but lots of people want the queen dead."

He wasn't wrong. Queen Evangeline had enemies, and some were right in her midst—like the ones who had encouraged her to pass laws that they later twisted against her.

In the end, the queen had discovered that she had less power than she'd thought—and now she wanted to change that. Merry intended to be right there when she succeeded. And as odd as it might seem to people who *didn't* know the Glass Queen, the queen wanted change, too. Sometimes it was hard for Merry to believe how close she had grown to Queen Evangeline.

Perhaps it was because they both knew what it was like to have people take advantage of you.

The night Merry first stole from the queen, guards had shoved her to the ground and she'd landed at the queen's feet.

"Do *not* mess with me!" Merry had shouted at them.

"It took me longer to learn to stand up for myself," the queen had said, then smiled at her. "I see you already understand it, though."

Merry was too angry to think about the fact that this was the *queen*. So she blurted out, "It's not that complicated. Everyone who has power shoves those of us who don't. I don't like it."

"No, I don't suppose you do." The queen studied her. Then she sent the guards away so they were alone. "Who wants to be a pawn?"

Merry had laughed. "I'm a *thief*, Your Majesty, and a *very* good one. I don't just steal for me, but for others who have less—"

"Then you shall become *my* thief. What do you say to going to school? Having security? A position at the palace eventually . . ."

"Why?"

"Because I realize I need help to make things right. The smallest ripples lead to great changes. Someone told me that years ago, and I'm starting to see the truth of it."

Merry wasn't exactly sure what the queen was talking about—but she had no doubts about the queen after that day. No matter who spoke against her, Meredith trusted the Glass Queen completely. Both the queen and her future Raven were going to gain power and put things right in their world.

CHAPTER 34

❖———❖———❖

Victoria

Although she didn't *feel* worry over Ida, Victoria checked on her injury as soon as she woke the next morning.

"Healing," Ida said. "I can hide it, Vic."

The shortened version of her name seemed strangely acceptable. It wasn't the name that her sisters had used, but it was softer than Victoria. Ida had earned the right to use it by getting injured at Victoria's side.

"Find me, or Algernon, if you need aid," Victoria said.

"You are a good friend," Ida answered.

Victoria frowned at her and left to meet with Meister Tik. He had been her mother's friend, as had Master Nightshade. It was logic that made her want to ask the combat master about her mother, about the secret, if the queen—or the queen's enemies—were responsible for her family's awful fate.

Victoria thought about the story she'd heard over and over while snuggled into her mother's side in her bed.

"Once there was a wicked queen. She was tall, and she was beautiful, but she was cold as the iciest wind." Vicky's mum paused;

she always paused here. Then she asked, "Do you know the worst part?"

Vicky did. She knew every word of the story, but she always said, "What?"

Her mother smiled. "There were once people who loved her. They would have done anything for her, but they died. All but one." She paused again, and then asked, "Do you know the biggest secret, the one the queen hid from everyone?"

"The world thought they were all gone," Vicky added. "No princesses. No princes. No kings. Just her."

"But the queen knew the secret," her mother said.

"There was a lost princess!"

Vicky's mother stroked her hair. "Yes. In one small house, in one small room, where a lot of boys and girls slept and lived, there was someone who was very happy. That one girl realized that she had to hide, though. She didn't want to be queen, or even a princess."

But Victoria still didn't know if the royal family died *because* of the queen—or if the queen was lucky. Did Queen Evangeline hide her cousin? Or was she lost and rediscovered? Was she wicked, or had she been, like Victoria, young and afraid because everyone she knew was suddenly dead?

Victoria had questions, and the more she thought about it, the more she realized that she wasn't going to be able to wait before starting to ask them. When she'd had her emotions removed, Victoria had made a plan: learn, wait, discover the villains. Without the pressure of grief or rage, that seemed possible.

Now she was already the subject of an attack on the streets of Glass City.

Now her roommate was injured.

Now she had met several obstinate kids who were determined to be her friends. Victoria knew that her family had been killed because of the secret—the one her parents knew, that Meister Tik and Master Nightshade knew, the one the queen herself knew.

Victoria realized that the fairy tale meant that the queen had hidden Kathleen Wardrop all those years ago, but was it to keep her safe? Had she begun inviting them to move to the castle earlier this year to protect them—or control them? Was she a villain . . . or just afraid?

Victoria thought about it. Again. She'd thought and thought since she'd learned who her mother was—who *she* was.

As she thought, she walked toward Meister Tik's combat rooms. She'd turned the corner when Meredith stepped out of an alcove. She'd somehow managed to look like she was intending on going to the palace rather than class.

"You look nice," Meredith said.

Victoria blinked. She was wearing one of the dresses Uncle Albert had ordered. Each one had a date tag, so she wore them in the order listed. "Good."

Meredith laughed, seeming friendlier than in the past. "You sound like the queen sometimes."

It was, of course, the exact wrong thing to say. Victoria tensed. Her hand drifted to the long case she carried over her shoulder. It was hand-cut and hand-sewn leather, warded to prevent intrusion by water, fire, or hands other than her own. It now held her new sword.

"I am not your enemy," Meredith whispered.

"You captured me."

"And you embarrassed me at court. Perhaps we could call a draw? A tie? And be *not*-enemies," Meredith said quietly. "We have common interests, Wardrop."

"The enemy of my enemy," Victoria pronounced, half in question.

Meredith grinned widely. "Yes."

The two walked in awkward silence to the combat room.

Inside, Meister Tik and another student were sparring. The boy had a rapier in one hand and a dagger in the other. Those weren't Victoria's preferred weapons, but in the boy's hands, they looked graceful.

"Less force, Charles." Meister Tik avoided a thrust and knocked the dagger away. "If you press too hard, you lose balance."

The boy executed an underarm cut that would've made contact if Meister Tik hadn't been wearing a protection ward.

"Or I distract you," Charles announced.

Meister Tik rewarded him with a smile. "Passable."

When he saw Victoria, the boy bowed to Meister Tik and asked, "May I stay?"

Tik shook his head. "I suppose that would be up to Victoria."

"I don't care who watches," Victoria admitted with a small shrug and a pointed look at Meredith, who now waited on a bench there. With her family gone, there was no need to pretend to be weaker than she was.

Victoria was ready to make a statement.

"Choose your weapon," Meister Tik said. "Meredith has offered to spar with you."

"Longsword." Victoria opened her case and unwrapped the leather bindings. She'd spent a good part of the night melding wards into the steel. When she wrapped her hand around the hilt, she felt the wards all sing.

Meredith obviously felt the surge, too. She raised a shield. Victoria flashed her a grin.

As Victoria drew her blade, it felt like an extension of her arm. No hand but hers could hold this sword without her consent.

"New blade?" Meister Tik asked.

"A gift from my parents," Victoria said, as if it were nothing. The sword was special, and not just because it was also an athame. It was the last gift from them. It would be the weapon she'd use to avenge their deaths.

Tik nodded and raised his combat wards. Holding such wards while fighting was a prerequisite to being a combat master, as was the ability to place those protection wards on one's pupils. The alternative was to practice with blunt swords.

Victoria walked toward Meister Tik and said, "I will dress my own wards. You may test them, but I will have no wards placed on me by others."

Her words were low, but both Charles and Meredith startled at them.

"The swords for the test aren't blunt," Meister Tik warned her. "If your wards fail—"

"I'll bleed." Victoria had practiced until her hand bled from clutching the athame. Carefully, she told Meister Tik, "I am never unwarded. *Ever.*"

Meredith silently lifted her sword, walked to the fight mat, and bowed.

Victoria bowed and lifted her sword into *vom Tag*. It was a standard high guard position, typically translated as "from the roof." Her sword was held back and high, enabling her to cut downward with force. It also enabled her to easily execute any of the five master cuts.

Without anything beyond a press at her wards to assure that they were, in fact, steady and present, Meister Tik gestured to them and said, "Begin."

Meredith struck. Not surprisingly, she immediately delivered a *Zwerchhau*, a horizontal cut that was good for breaking a high guard.

That strike left Meredith in, more or less, the guard *Ochs*—where the sword jutted forward like the horn of an ox—so Victoria struck with a *Krumphau*. The crooked strike was one that was a fit for the *Ochs* guard.

And so they went, striking, parrying, and moving. That was the other key in fighting with the blade: one had to think of the right answering cut or guard while moving. It was, as had often been said, a lot like the steps of a dance or the customs of a formal conversation. Some moves simply beckoned others.

After the sixth cut, Meredith faltered.

Victoria's blade would have pierced her throat if she hadn't been warded. Instead, the tip of Victoria's longsword glanced off her as soon as it touched.

"Well done!" Tik said approvingly. "You will join my third-level course with Ida and Meredith once you are eligible to test again. For now, Miss Wardrop, you may join the second-year class."

Victoria and Meredith exchanged another bow, and in that moment, Victoria decided that perhaps the other girl wasn't all bad. Allies were welcome, and perhaps Meredith would turn out to be one, too.

CHAPTER 35

Milan

The next morning, Milan was feeling guilty about both his lies and meeting the queen. He was halfway to the dining hall when he finally asked Algernon, "Where were you last night?"

"Steel Close," Algernon said, with the same sort of tone he used to talk about the Netherwhere.

Milan grabbed his arm. "Weapons Alley? She took you to *Weapons Alley*? What was she thinking? What were *you* thinking?"

Algernon shook his friend's hand off. "That she needed me . . . And where were *you*?"

Milan sighed. "I went into the city with Meredith."

At first, Algernon said nothing. He walked silently through the hall, not remarking, as he had previously, on Milan's obvious tendencies to look to alcoves or shadowed doorways. Eventually, he said, "If you don't want to do something, tell me. Don't lie."

Milan looked down. He couldn't argue with Algernon. "I

wanted to see Florie." He paused, then whispered, "Head of my old thief house."

Algernon looked sad. "I'd have gone with you if you'd asked. You went to the Netherwhere with me."

"Next time," Milan swore. "And I won't lie about where I'm going."

Algernon opened his mouth to say something else, but someone bumped into him. Then they got swept up in the students filling the classroom.

Like many of the classrooms, it felt old. The room had rows of desks, heavy wooden things that were polished by years of students' hands. A slate was mounted to the wall, although he'd yet to see a teacher use it.

Milan slipped into an empty desk only moments before the teacher marched to the front of the class. They all stared as she sketched a quick rune and her name floated in the air to her left side in bold letters: DUCHESS SALTWYCHE. She hadn't said much at the group meeting, but everything about her was striking, from her entrance to the closed fan that dangled from her wrist.

And since Milan had stolen such fans before, he knew it was a weapon. The longer he was here, the less he thought Corvus was actually *safe* at all. He had a sinking feeling that he was going to hate this class.

As Duchess Saltwyche walked, she announced, "There are more ways to manipulate the student next to you than there are to poison him, more ways to control her than there are to stab her. In my classes these next several years, you will learn how to read both fears and interests." She turned quickly on her heel and faced them. Her bustle didn't so much as sway as she did so. "And you will learn to *exploit* them."

Milan wrote down what she'd said, and then sat with pen and parchment at the ready.

"What is it you want most?" Duchess Saltwyche fixed her gaze on several of the students.

One girl met her look and smiled. A boy in a suit that was fine enough to scream *money* crossed his arms. Both of them received a slight nod. Then she looked at Victoria.

Instead of dodging the teacher's question, Victoria answered, "That's none of your concern."

The room grew even more silent.

"That, children, is the wrong response." Duchess Saltwyche walked toward Victoria.

"It's not wrong." Victoria didn't raise her voice. "If I choose not to share, you cannot use it against me. Not to control me. Not to influence me. It's a rebuttal that you cannot overcome."

Milan heard the entire room draw a collective breath. It was like at the introduction meeting, but this time she was challenging a *teacher*. It was bad enough to question an adult, but a teacher?

He coughed.

When Victoria opened her mouth again, he coughed louder. She glanced at him and pressed her lips together, as if he had done something wrong. Algernon, however, sent him a relieved look.

Duchess Saltwyche looked pointedly at Victoria and said, "Understanding motives helps one work past their emotions."

"So do elixirs," Victoria said mildly, sparking a ripple of laughter across the room.

Duchess Saltwyche's composure slipped. "You remind me of your father."

"Thank you."

The duchess continued. "We were students at the same time, and I disliked him. He was never loyal to the crown, if you ask me."

Victoria stood. "Has anyone *asked* you? Someone murdered him recently, you know." She sounded perfectly calm, despite the fact that she was utterly dismissing their teacher's authority. "I'm hoping to find the culprits. Maybe starting with a list of people who disliked him is a good first step."

Duchess Saltwyche gasped. "Out! Out of my classroom!"

"Excellent demonstration," Victoria said. "You *clearly* want power."

She walked out, and after a brief pause, Milan scrambled out of his seat and followed her into the hall. Algernon was a second faster.

Milan wanted to learn, but he'd rather take a few low marks or even demerits than abandon someone who was grieving her murdered parents.

"I can't believe she said that!" Algernon's voice carried loudly.

Some other students were headed to midday meal. Milan pushed through them to catch up with Victoria and Algernon, who was doggedly at her side already.

"Are we friends, Milan?" she asked.

Beside her, Algernon smothered a smile.

"Excuse me?" Milan asked.

"You coughed to distract her and protect me," Victoria said baldly. "But you did not join us last night."

"I had things to do," Milan said.

"Spying on Meredith," Algernon added helpfully.

Victoria smiled. "Allies, then."

They stood awkwardly for a moment. Milan wanted to explain that Merry wasn't all bad, but he wasn't sure Victoria or Algernon would listen.

"How is Ida?" Algernon asked.

"Healing." Victoria pressed her lips tightly together.

"From what?" Milan asked.

"Poisoned sword." Algernon flashed him a smile. "We had an adventure—not quite the Netherwhere, but exciting."

Milan wasn't sure Algernon realized what he'd said, but Victoria certainly did. She stared at him intently and asked, "Do you know a chimera, by any chance?"

"A what?" Meredith asked from somewhere behind Victoria.

Milan snagged Algernon by the arm while he was opening and closing his mouth. No one was supposed to be able to go to the Netherwhere the way Algernon did—and announcing his secret so publicly seemed worse than dangerous.

Victoria scowled but didn't follow as Milan all but dragged Algernon away like a lifeless sack of turnips and called out, "We'll see you at dinner, Vicky! Merry!"

CHAPTER 36

◆————◆————◆

Meredith

T hose boys are peculiar," Merry said quietly as she and Victoria watched them scurry away.

"Obviously, they *do* know a chimera," Victoria added.

Milan was shrewd to act to protect Algernon. Merry respected him more for it. This was part of what made thieves such good Ravens: they were fiercely loyal.

She turned toward Victoria and couldn't help but stare at her, as she realized for the first time that the girl in front of her, the one the queen was so interested in, looked a lot like paintings of the Glass Queen as a girl. A certain slant of light, and Victoria's dark eyes could have been looking from those same paintings. Victoria *had* to be related to the queen some way. Lady Wardrop's incredible talents and Victoria's gift with wards and swords suddenly made sense.

"Why are you watching me?" Victoria asked.

Merry deflected her question. "Why was Milan watching me?"

"You're in the wrong house," Victoria started. "You should be in with the ward workers. You're good."

"Thank you." Merry paused before adding, "I am not your enemy, Victoria Wardrop."

Victoria met her gaze calmly and asked, "Whose enemy are you?"

"I'm here for myself," Merry said honestly. "I want to be able to sleep somewhere safe, learn how to work wards, and not be hungry. If being your ally will make that happen, that's what I am."

"You make more sense than most people here," Victoria said as she turned to walk away.

"I think being your ally would be a better choice than being your enemy," Merry called after her.

Victoria paused, smiled widely, and said, "You may be right."

After she left, Merry waited just long enough to turn into an unused passage to make her way out of the school. She wasn't scheduled to see the queen—especially in the middle of the day—but she knew the queen would want to hear that there was talk of chimeras. That meant whatever was going on involved the Netherwhere.

People feared kelpies, and far too often they captured faeries, and no one quite knew what to think of the ever-watching gargoyles.

If the chimera decided to come through the World Door, according to the queen's advisors they were all doomed. They'd even convinced the queen to ban travel to the Netherwhere— and not go there herself anymore.

But the queen had hinted to Meredith that she wasn't sure what the advisors said was true. She hadn't ever said outright that her advisors might be treacherous, but Merry was increasingly sure that the real threats to the Glass Empire were in the queen's court. Not chimeras. Not gargoyles. The *real* threats were the men who threatened stability, stirring wars and whispering lies.

Either way, though, the queen should know the news of the Netherwhere. Carefully, quietly, and quickly, Meredith slipped outside the Corvus School for the Artfully Inclined and headed toward the Glass Castle to update the queen.

CHAPTER 37

◆────◆────◆

Victoria

Victoria was surprised to find herself trusting Meredith. She thought about it as she was walking. Her plan had been to protect herself from grief but not allow anyone else close again. Ever. But that plan hadn't accounted for other kids like Algernon or Milan. Or now . . . Meredith.

A gargoyle that was perched on a window summoned Victoria closer with a toss of her sharp beak.

"*Ripples,*" it whispered in her mind.

She walked to where the creature had directed her, and there Victoria found a secret passageway hidden behind a ward. She disabled it and slipped into the shadowed hallway.

"If Wardrop doesn't want to go to the castle, we're not sending her," Meister Tik snapped.

"And are *you* suddenly in charge of the Glass Empire, Tik? When did you receive such authority?"

Victoria came around a corner, tucked herself into the shadows, and watched the headmaster rub his mostly bald head irritably.

"She's a child, Horatio."

"These children are all being trained to *serve* the crown and empire." Headmaster Edwards folded his arms. "She will do as she's told. They all will."

Victoria dropped her wards enough that they both saw her. The headmaster furrowed his brow. "Miss Sweeney—"

"Wardrop is fine." Victoria nodded. "If I am able to break wards, I find it useful to test myself. It's a game Mama and I played. Yours are passable wards, Headmaster."

The headmaster frowned. "You cannot go around disassembling wards, child."

"I actually can, sir. I can't always do complicated layered ones as quickly." Victoria paused. "And sometimes just closed doors are good, too. Not exactly *wards*, but they muffle voices."

Before Horatio could launch into a lecture, Victoria asked, "What is it that the Glass Queen wants of me?"

"The queen never *wants* things, Miss Wardrop. She orders them. I will accompany you to the Glass Castle." The headmaster pressed his lips together, and she was reminded painfully of the way her mother had spoken his name. She was not going *anywhere* with him.

Meister Tik's hand was on the hilt of his side sword, and she guessed he mistrusted the headmaster as much as her parents had.

"Unfortunately, I am in mourning, sir. Such social engagements are not suitable."

The headmaster gaped at her. "Miss Wardrop! Your duty is—"

"There are rules, sir," Victoria said, cutting him off. Without meaning to do so, she pulled a surge of ley energy into herself so fiercely that both men stumbled.

"How many athames are you holding?" Headmaster Edwards asked.

"Such answers are not required by any guideline in the school manual."

"Victoria," said a voice behind her.

Master Nightshade stood there, his peculiar gas mask perched atop his head. He looked a bit like an actual raven with a misplaced beak.

"You were to be meeting me, Miss Sweeney," he said.

"Nightshade," the headmaster began, "we were just discussing—"

"I have a schedule, Horatio. If Miss Sweeney had made an appointment with *you* first, I would return to my laboratory. But there are things that our esteemed queen requires of me, and as I'm required to *teach* this year and complete my duties, I must attend to a schedule."

Victoria caught sight of the relief in Meister Tik's eyes, so she said nothing contrary. There was no meeting, but the alchemist was offering her an excuse to walk away from the headmaster without Meister Tik drawing his blade. They weren't her family, but they were the next best thing, and her parents had trusted them.

Master Nightshade reached up to scratch his head, grinned, and pulled off his mask. "I knew I left that mask somewhere!"

Then he extended the mask to Victoria and said, "Come now, we are behind schedule."

Victoria bowed slightly to the headmaster, bowed deeply to Meister Tik, and walked away with the alchemist.

They rounded a corner and stopped at the mouth of a narrow passageway that hadn't been there previously. Master Nightshade ordered, "Go. Quickly, now."

Victoria stepped inside.

Once there, the alchemist glanced at her and mouthed, "Ward us."

Mutely, she did so.

The tunnel appeared to be cut out of salt. Immense clear, white, and pale-pink crystals jutted out all around them, making walking more challenging. The crystals on the ground had obviously been harvested to make the floor level.

The opening behind them sealed so they were enclosed, and Nightshade said, "Tik summoned me. He didn't want you going anywhere with the headmaster."

"Nor did I," Victoria pronounced. "Or would I!"

"Good. Good," Master Nightshade said, nodding at her. "I haven't trusted the queen for years, but I believe she actually cared for your family. The one I distrust is Horatio. He's up to something, and I don't know if the queen truly summoned you. If she wanted you, why not send Ravens to fetch you?" The alchemist met her gaze. "The only *real* answer, since we don't know whom to trust, is to simply not be here. To vanish."

"Run away? If I go to Uncle Albert's, I'll be found. I am still a *child*, so where would you have me go, Master Nightshade? Help me."

"I am trying," he told her. "Thieves know the city. My *son* travels with a thief. Talk to Milan. I brought him here to help."

"I know you cured me—"

"It will wear off," he blurted out. And while Victoria was looking at him in vague horror, he added, "Ask my son to take you to meet Ebba. Tell Ebba what you know."

"Ebba? That's the chimera, right?"

The alchemist nodded. "The headmaster likes power. For some reason, he wanted you here. Your mother was groomed to be Evangeline's guard, and I think there were more than a few who realized who she really was. Ev protected her secrets. I've brewed medicinals to silence more than one person who would have hurt your mother . . . and I've done so at the queen's command."

"So, she is used to killing for power?"

"Yes." The alchemist shook his head. "But that doesn't mean—"

"I understand. I'm not expecting *all* the answers today," Victoria said softly.

For a moment, there was silence, but then Master Nightshade added, "The queen is very familiar with the medicine I gave you. She asked me to brew more of it years *before* your family died. Said we'd likely need the medicine one day, and I should 'fix' it in case one of you needed it. I have no idea if she was intending for me to change it or if she is guilty, too, but . . . I . . . Kat was my friend. I did what I had to do for her. I changed the formula because your mother was as a *sister* to me . . . Now go. Ask my son to take you to meet Ebba."

CHAPTER 38

◆———◇———◆

Victoria

Victoria went directly to the boys' dormitory, pounded on the door, and told the boy there, "Fetch Nightshade."

When Algernon appeared, she said, "I need to meet Ebba. Preferably now."

Milan poked his head around the side of Algernon's suddenly motionless body. "Do you want to come in?"

Victoria shook her head. "No. Follow me. My dorm is safe, and I need my swords before we leave."

"Leave?" Algernon echoed. "We're leaving?"

She nodded. "Master Nightshade says—"

"What?"

"Master Nightshade—"

"My father?"

"Yes. Let me finish. Master Nightshade, the Queen's Alchemist, your father, my mother's friend, the man who removed my shadow—"

"He did what?" Milan interrupted as the boys stepped into

the hall. The heavy door slammed shut behind them as they scrambled to keep up with her.

"I *told* you he cured my grief," she said. Victoria made herself slow down. She glanced at the boys, took a calming breath, and spoke quietly, "He removed my shadow to get rid of my grief. And now he has told me that you could take me to Ebba, who might have some answers to all this."

"*Now?*"

"Yes. Right now. The headmaster wanted to take me to see the queen, but I think he may have killed my family—"

"*What?* Slow down, please." Milan reached out like he would grab her arm. His fingers barely grazed her skin, but it was enough to cause her wards to activate. Milan was thrown backward. He thunked against a wall and slid to the ground.

"My wards cover my body," Victoria explained, looking down at him. "Touching me isn't typically a good plan."

"You think?" Milan pushed to his feet, hand cradling the back of his head.

For a long moment, they all stood in silence, students passing.

The buzz of voices lifted all around them. Attention wasn't what they needed, and who knew who was lurking nearby.

"Move along," Milan grumbled at the watchers. "I fell. It's not that interesting."

"Your father said my mother was as a sister to him," Victoria said in a low voice. "And I know we were on your manor grounds, Algernon. And Nightshade pointed out that you"—she nodded at Milan—"can lead me into the city if we cannot go to the Netherwhere just now."

For a moment, Algernon was speechless.

"Your father, and I, believe that either the queen is *responsible* for killing my family or *she* is in danger," Victoria said, finally letting the words out.

No one, least of all a small girl, could fight a queen—let alone one protected by Ravens. If she *was* responsible, what could a few kids do? If she *wasn't* guilty, they were equally unprepared. Could Victoria actually protect the queen as her mother once had?

How was Victoria to know which was true?

The boys were still staring at her, and Victoria realized it was a lot of information all at once. She walked away, leading them into the Talhoffer dormitory. The dorm was still within the school—where they might be in peril—but inside it were her weapons.

Victoria wasn't safe at Corvus—or possibly anywhere in the entire empire.

Don't trust the headmaster, Nightshade had said. Her parents and Tik had also given her reasons to doubt him, her mother and father in words, and Meister Tik when he'd looked ready to draw a weapon.

Victoria had to leave Corvus today.

Now.

"This way," Victoria said, leading them to a corner of the common room. As they walked, she looked for Ida, and the boys followed without arguing.

"I'd rather you don't die," Victoria whispered to them.

"Oh, me too!" Milan agreed. "So let's skip the dying part, eh?"

Victoria paused and looked around. Ida wasn't there in the common room, so no one else spoke.

She led the boys into a quiet corner and said, "Sit."

The boys exchanged a look.

"I need to get my weapons."

"We're coming," Algernon said.

Victoria sighed. "Boys may not enter girls' bedrooms, Nightshade." She pointed to a pair of chairs beside them against a darkened wall. They were empty. "Sit. I'll be quick."

Milan shook his head. "We are about to break a lot more rules than which rooms we can go in."

Victoria couldn't argue.

Algernon gently said, "We are leaving together." He looked at Milan. "Either into the city or into the Netherwhere."

Victoria led the two boys into her room as she gathered her things. She took a minute to look around. She had thought she'd be staying for a few years.

"We can come back," Algernon said.

"After we commit treason?" Milan scoffed. "Or confirm that the headmaster is the one to fear? I don't think so."

It dawned on Victoria how much they were all risking. She thought of Meredith's goals: a home, knowledge, and food. Victoria wanted the same things, and imagined the boys did, too.

Life. Safety. Freedom. A home.

It was exactly what her parents had fought for, and Victoria felt very much like their daughter in that moment.

CHAPTER 39

◆——◆——◆

Algernon

Walking through the halls of the school with a thief and a ward-working fighter only emphasized how little Algernon knew beyond alchemy and plants. He simply wasn't made for stealth, hadn't been trained in it. Milan moved like the thief he was, and Victoria already seemed like a warrior.

Then a tiny creature darted into his line of sight and darted away. She did so again. The second time she swooped near, she spoke to him. "Come. Pen'lpee knows the path. Ebba waiting."

"Is that the headmaster's dragon?" Victoria asked.

"Dragonet," Algernon corrected.

"We have to keep moving. The headmaster will be looking for me," Victoria reminded him. "If the dragonet tells him where we are—"

The tiny dragonet spit a plume of fire in her direction.

Victoria's wards were constant, though. The fire bounced off her, scattering in smoke and ashes. It was beautiful, but far too attention-getting.

"It's all right," Algernon said. "She's leading us to safety."

Milan and Victoria exchanged a doubtful look, but they still followed him. It reminded him of being with his brother, and he wondered briefly if that was what it had been like for Victoria and her sisters. Were friends just another sort of family?

Penelope darted in and out of his line of sight, zipping so high up that all that he saw was a flash of smoke or blink of fire.

"Are you sure we can trust her?" Victoria asked.

The little zip of a dragonet was so fast that Milan jumped back. She hovered in front of his face. Then she stared into Victoria's eyes.

And then in his mind, Algernon heard her as loud as any creature, much louder than something so small. "Yes, yes, yes," Penelope trilled, and then she was gone again.

"It appears so," he said.

"I heard her, too," Victoria said. "Like with gargoyles."

"Same," Milan said very quietly.

Decision made, they took off, faster than before, chasing Penelope. But when the dragonet led them to the sixth floor and suddenly vanished through a window, Algernon, Milan, and Victoria all skidded to a stop.

"Are you sure?" Milan asked hesitantly. "The street is a long way down if we're wrong."

"It will be fine," Algernon said. "Trust me."

"You? Definitely. But not the dragonet," Milan said.

"What if it only works for the headmaster?" Victoria asked.

"We lack *wings*," Milan said. "We're several floors up, we're going to break bones. Maybe *die*."

Victoria looked out the window. "Guys? There's no dragonet out there now."

"I've gone through upper-floor doorways before," Algernon said carefully. "I've always landed on the ground of the Netherwhere."

"After a fall?" Milan prompted.

"No. Time and space move differently when you enter the Netherwhere." Algernon wanted to be patient, reminded himself to do so, because the things most people knew of the Netherwhere wouldn't fill a teacup. "If you're afraid, we can go into the city instead. We can work our way to Nightshade Manor and use *that* passageway."

Instead of replying, Milan looked at Victoria for her answer.

"In the city, there are Ravens, adults, kelpies. Threats. Getting to Nightshade Manor seems slow." Victoria looked at the window as she spoke. "Open it. I'll go through here. Now."

Milan shrugged. "It's not the worst plan ever."

And Algernon felt for the space that would fold back, air shifting, time changing. It was like a handle made of nothing—different yet again from the last few trips to the Netherwhere. He found it, snagged it with an outstretched hand, and tugged.

"Go," he urged.

Milan went first, climbing into the window frame and then falling into nothingness.

Victoria, sword held in her hand as if nervous about who or what they'd meet upon landing, followed.

Algernon hoped she didn't accidentally tumble into Milan and stab him.

Then Algernon hoisted himself into the casement and let go.

In the space between one blink and the next, Algernon was facedown on what appeared to be a forest floor. One booted foot was hanging in the empty air, as if it were caught on the window frame, and behind him, about waist-high from the ground, blinked the image of the hall where they'd just been.

With a grin, Algernon tugged his foot through the blinking doorway and pushed himself to his feet. Pine needles clung to him from ankle to chin.

"W'come home," something said.

It could have been a dragonet, or a faery, or even a gargoyle. It could have been one of the shy creatures who were often no more than a flash of eyes in the shadows. It didn't matter. There was a rush of joy in him, a peace that washed over him at being where he belonged. But it was accompanied by a rush of worry for his brother—worry fed by knowing that whoever was responsible for the Wardrop family's death wasn't likely to be particularly fond of those who helped Victoria vanish.

First things came first. He had to introduce Victoria to Ebba, and then he'd go home to see to Alistair's safety.

"Let's find Ebba," Algernon announced. The rest of the challenges would follow.

CHAPTER 40

Victoria

The Netherwhere looked like an ordinary forest, which simply happened to be accessed by going through a window. As Algernon had promised, they'd landed in a safe space. Moss, leaves, and pine needles had cushioned their fall. He hadn't mentioned, however, that the air would be thicker and breathing would be harder.

While Algernon was untangling himself, Victoria stood with her sword clutched in hand, seeking a threat. That simple act felt laborious, as if she had to push through taffy to get her sword drawn and raised.

Algernon and Milan looked fine. Dirty, but uninjured.

Victoria felt odd, but she thought it was the air in this world. It *couldn't* be worry or fear. If Victoria had still felt *that*, she couldn't have stepped out that window. It was remarkable that the boys had done so. They were both here, though, alive and intact. And she hadn't been forced to go anywhere with a headmaster who, according to Master Nightshade, was most likely responsible for the loss of her family.

"We need to find the chimera," she said, reminding the boys but also testing her ability to speak.

The air had, as she'd suspected, made her words slower. Victoria wasn't sure she'd want to swing a sword in such a place. Fighting required breathing, and she had her doubts about her ability to do both well in the Netherwhere.

Still holding her sword—which was, of course, also an athame—Victoria began to reach out in search of ley lines, in case she needed to draw wards. That didn't require the same sort of breathing as sword fighting did.

Algernon motioned for them to walk, and Victoria stood on one side as Milan stood on his other side. Before they'd all taken three steps, a massive creature came galloping toward them. She could swear the ground trembled at its approach.

Both boys paused. Milan stepped slightly back, letting Algernon walk a few steps forward to face the creature.

The chimera!

As it slowed, three heads peered around—either curiously or menacingly; Victoria wasn't quite sure which it was. It assessed them with eyes of serpent, goat, and lion.

"Ebba," Algernon greeted the chimera cheerfully.

"Greetings," Ebba's first head, a lion, said to him, but in a blink, it turned so that it stared at Milan. "You smell of *her*."

"Of . . ." Algernon also stared.

The snake part of Ebba hissed and darted forward with fangs exposed, as if to bite Milan.

Victoria lifted her sword in warning. "He is my friend."

"Is a friend who walks with your enemy a friend?" the lion head asked.

The serpent kept hissing and darting at her as if it could startle her into moving out of its path. So one head was serious, and another was trying to bite. Maybe having several heads at once meant you could feel many feelings at once.

"Milan?"

"I can explain why," the thief said. "I was out with Merry, and we ran into the queen . . ."

Victoria didn't care. She was here to see the chimera, and arguing about what Milan smelled of or why he smelled seemed unimportant. She stepped closer to the chimera and asked, "Are you the only one of your kind in this world?"

All three heads turned to her. As one voice, they said, "We are the only chimera in *any* world. One form of three minds. We are *the* chimera."

Victoria nodded, but she still did not sheathe her sword. Knowing that the chimera was a friend of her mother's didn't make it any easier to face the mighty, ferocious-looking creature. Admittedly, *goats* weren't the most frightening things ever, but lions and serpents were. Even a nonvenomous serpent had fangs. Lions, of course, had strong jaws, and the ability to eat terrified children.

"These are my allies," Victoria told the chimera, but she said it loudly—just in case any other creature lurked nearby and meant them harm. She would protect the boys. They'd come here to aid *her*, and that meant they were owed her protection.

"The Night human is *my* human," Ebba said. Their heads nodded, although the goat nodded last. "But this one"—the snake head extended like an arm, pointing at Milan—"smells of queen."

"Meredith took me . . . We met the queen in the city." Milan looked unwell. "Meredith stole a garnet, and the queen gave me one."

"Give us the stone," the lion head of Ebba roared, and the snake head started hissing.

As they spoke, gargoyles came; faeries and several dragonets also eased nearer.

"I swear I am not your enemy," Milan said, looking between Algernon and Victoria.

Victoria nodded, glancing at the creatures who were watching. She wasn't sure why they were gathering, but it made her relax and feel happy in a way she hadn't since her family had died. Was it the presence of so many gargoyles at once that brought feelings back—or that enough time had passed for her to feel things other than grief and rage? Or maybe she was feeling so much because the boys were there. Friends. People who were there to help her find the vile person who'd taken away her family.

And a chimera. *The* chimera. The rather terrifying chimera. But her mother said to trust the chimera.

"Stone," Algernon repeated, not sounding as hesitant as he often did.

Milan fished a sparkling red stone from his pocket. The goat extended a dripping tongue and licked it out of Milan's hand. They chewed the jewel loudly, staring at the children as they did so.

"Why doesn't the queen trust you? And why *did* my mother?" Victoria asked the chimera.

"The queen used to. She was once afraid. She had a shadow

then." Ebba's lion head began to tell the story. "But her family was gone, and she was afraid. The young Evangeline needed power. Safety. A way to protect her cousin—and herself. A way to rule without fear, or grief, or worry."

"What happened?" Victoria asked.

"She could come here then, but her grief was large. Then she gave up her shadow, and they made her like them. She came no more."

Ebba's lion head stopped for a minute to roar. Then they continued. "She trusted others instead of *me*! Do not trust the men who whisper to the queen."

"Like the headmaster," Milan said.

"Yes!" Ebba nodded. "And others."

"The queen's entire family died . . . Like mine?" Victoria asked.

"She had one cousin who lived," Ebba said. "Evangeline sent the girl to a house of thieves to hide her. You know *that* story, Vicky."

All three of Ebba's heads were watching Victoria. The serpent third was swaying in a way that was almost hypnotic. Victoria was silent, hands on the hilt of her sword. Yes, she knew part of this story—that her mother was the missing child. But the fact that the queen had no shadow either was news to her.

"Lady Wardrop?" Milan whispered. "That means . . ."

"No. The *whole* royal family was killed," Algernon said. "Our enemies from across the water came, and they killed everyone but our queen. All of the books said so. The papers."

"They were wrong," Ebba's lion voice rumbled. "Evangeline,

the young queen-to-be, was tossed aside with the dead. When she saw that Kat was alive, too, the queen shoved her into a laundry chute to hide her."

The goat head let out a bleating sort of wail.

"You're Kat's daughter, and she was . . . so you're . . . the princess?" Milan kneeled.

Ebba's three heads all nodded. The serpent swayed rapidly and hissed in little bursts, like a cheer. The goat head stretched out, as if to rub against Victoria.

The lion head spoke again. "The heir. Daughter of the Thief Princess, child of Ward and Weapon, the Hidden Knife. Shadowless now, like the fragile Glass Queen."

"My father has to know . . . but I had no idea," Algernon said.

"Your father was a friend to my mother," Victoria said quietly. "He knew. Meister Tik. Probably Uncle Albert. Maybe more people . . . And the gargoyles. They know everything."

She looked up at the gargoyles. Immediately, several gargoyles flew closer. Wings clattered, and after a moment, Victoria reached out with the hand that didn't hold the blade.

She looked at Algernon and Milan. "My mother was lucky to have good friends, and I am lucky to have *you*."

She glanced at the chimera. "I need my shadow back, don't I?"

"Yes, and *she* does too," the lion head said. "But . . . they gave the queen girl the potion. Without her feelings, she'd listen to them. She heard their lies as truth and shut us out. She froze her heart."

"Feelings are necessary. They are how we know different is

not ba-a-a-d," the goat added with a long bleating noise and a loud burp. "Hurting is part of healing."

"But queen let them give her poison," the snake hissed.

Victoria reached out again, keeping a hand on the wing of one gargoyle after the next. Tears were leaking from her eyes, and she sniffled loudly.

When the crowd of gargoyles and faeries parted, the most amazing thing happened.

There—so realistic that Victoria thought she must be dreaming—were her sisters.

"How . . ." Victoria shook her head. "Are you showing me their spirits or—"

"No." All three of Ebba's voices lifted together in unmistakable pride and joy. "They are here. Rupert brought them to us."

"Vicky?" a small voice said.

"Lizzie?" Victoria stared. "But I thought you were all dead . . . Our parents, and you and Alice . . ."

Lizzie grabbed her in a tight hug. "Not us. We had to stay hidden. It wasn't safe."

Alice pointed at the boy with them. "He is All-stairs!"

The boy, Alistair, grinned as both Algernon and Milan hugged him. "I woke up at home today, and then a bunch of gargoyles showed up. You know how they stalk me."

Victoria was only half listening. She had a sword still in one hand, but she now had her baby sister on her hip. Her older sister was on the other side of baby Alice, and for a moment it was just like normal: they were protecting Alice as the world went on around them.

"Gargoyles?" Milan echoed.

"We *all* got here by gargoyle flight." The younger Night-shade, Alistair, motioned to a group of boys who were now chasing faeries and whooping. "The old man sent a whole flock of gargoyles to the house today."

"Nightshade?" Victoria asked. "He sent gargoyles to . . . rescue you."

"And us," Lizzie said quietly. "Back when the bad men came to our house, the gargoyles grabbed us and brought us here."

"I thought . . . I couldn't." Victoria felt tears track down her face. "I couldn't open the door, Lizzie. I was too afraid after I saw Mama and Poppa, and . . ."

"We're here," Lizzie reminded her. "Right here. Safe."

Victoria couldn't say anything else. She squeezed her baby sister, and Lizzie hugged her. Together, they held Alice as tightly as she would allow.

"The stone ones brought the children here," Ebba said quietly. "You were not in the warded room, heir."

Victoria looked at the chimera. "You watched over them?"

The chimera grinned and nodded with all three heads.

"I am sorry we could not save Kat this time," the lion head rumbled. "Many times, we did. This time, we failed."

"The gargoyles have always watched over Kathleen and the alchemist and their children," Ebba said. "Even though the Nightshade boys—ahem—sometimes resisted their guards."

The Nightshade brothers exchanged a guilty look.

"Queen resists our help," said the snake head. "Bad queen!"

"Down, Vicky," Alice insisted suddenly. "Put me down!" Alice squirmed out of Victoria's arms and ran to pat the lion's great face.

"It's all right. She's safe," Lizzie whispered to Victoria. "Ebba *adores* her."

"Safe here," the snake head hissed loudly. "We watch children. *Promised*."

"Thank you," Victoria said. There was so much to figure out, but it was different now. She had her sisters. That was everything. It made her want to stay, but something tickled her thoughts. There was at least one more person in her family, someone else who might be hurting, and if the gargoyles guarded her, too . . .

Ebba stretched and yawned as Alice climbed up their back and started brushing their mane. "All of these children are tiring."

"Everyone could just stay here forever," Lizzie suggested.

"Here," the goat head said. They extended their tongue. On it was a crumble of red dust from the jewel they'd chewed and crushed.

The snake head hissed, and what looked like boiled spit covered the red jewel dust.

"Take this," Ebba's lion head ordered. "It will not return all of your shadow at once, but little by little, your shadow will find you and join you after you take the antidote."

It looked far from appealing. Sizzling and sparkling, covered in venom, the gem dust didn't seem like something she ought to swallow.

"Remember. Trust the chimera," Milan whispered.

Victoria reached out, lifted a sticky glob of it, and popped it into her mouth. Not shockingly, it burned all the way down. Goat spit and crushed gems didn't turn into candy, apparently.

She had no sooner swallowed the last bit that was stuck to her teeth than she felt it—feelings coming back. Not everything, but she felt excited, and friendly, and in the middle, she felt hopeful. She smiled at them, all of them, her friends, and her sisters, and the chimera. "I *like* you."

The lion and snake heads laughed. The goat's head still had a tongue full of sparkling, sticky medicine, so it smiled open-mouthed but did not laugh.

Her older sister smiled, and baby Alice said, "Like you, too, Vicky!"

Algernon scooped the rest of the medicine into a jar he'd pulled out of some pocket or other. Sounding very grown-up, he said, "You can't go taking this all at once. You'll need to do it in bites."

"You're a good friend," Vicky told him.

"No girl slobber or hugs!" Algernon warned.

She stuck out her tongue. Then she looked at Ebba, switching her gaze from one head to the next as she asked, "The antidote . . . do I need *all* of it? And is there a time limit?"

The three-headed creature smiled at her. "You are wise."

"What are we going to do?" Algernon asked quietly.

"I can't stay here," Vicky said. "*They* should, and you can, but I need to see my cousin."

"Nightshades, apparently, help the royals, so . . ." Algernon shook his head before adding, "I go where you go."

Milan nodded. "Well, I'm certainly not going to stay here and braid Ebba's mane. I'm going with you, too."

Alice patted Ebba's heads. "I wait with big kitty. I braid."

Lizzie smiled at Alice and gave Vicky a hug. "You go ahead."

"To the manor first?" Algernon asked. "Alistair is safe here with your sisters, and once we get there, we can fetch my father and make a plan."

Vicky shook her head. "No, I'm going directly to the palace now. It's time to speak to the queen."

The boys looked at her as if she had lost her mind.

"Apparently, Victoria got impulsiveness back in her first batch of feelings," Milan said.

"Why couldn't it be silliness first? Or cautiousness?" Algernon added.

Vicky grinned. "Wait till I get fearlessness back . . ."

The boys shuddered.

"Come on," Vicky urged.

She wanted answers. The queen had them. So Vicky was going to go get them—and if she was lucky, she would cure the queen, too.

CHAPTER 41

Algernon

Algernon had always expected to meet the queen. Eventually. But he hadn't expected to be taking her a gift of goat spit.

"Victoria?" he asked carefully.

"You can call me Vicky now," she said.

"Right. *Vicky* . . . Is this really the best idea?" Algernon tried to keep his worries out of his voice. "What if you're wrong? What if *she* is the . . . the *enemy*?"

"You don't need to come with me," she said bluntly, as usual, but with an unfamiliar edge of fear in *her* voice, too. "I'm pretty sure she's innocent, and I think she'll be fine once we give her the antidote." She smiled. "All I need is a gate from here to somewhere near the palace . . . Or a guide if we need to go through the city streets."

Algernon reminded himself that sometimes the things that weren't fights were important, too. Milan could guide them through the city, and Algernon could open or find gates. They weren't Ravens yet. They were kids. Together, though, they had strength, stealth, and the ability to open doors.

"We stick together." He said the words as soon as he thought them. "Let's go."

Maybe he was being impulsive too, but how often had he felt braver just because he had a thief at his side in the Netherwhere? Having a friend at your side made everything a little less scary.

All three of Ebba's heads grinned, and a gate opened up— over the sea.

Algernon glanced at the chimera.

"Horsesss," the snake end of Ebba hissed, dragging the word out.

"I'm ready," Vicky announced.

"We're really riding kelpies?" Algernon asked. "Any tips?"

"Hold on," said the goat head, with a snorting, laughing sound.

Algernon nodded, and Milan looked horrified. Vicky, however, simply leaped through the gate. Algernon watched as she splashed into the sea.

Before he could ask anything else, Ebba nudged him and Milan through the air. They both plopped down into the empty water. Victoria was already bobbing there, and Algernon was really hoping that he hadn't been wrong to trust the chimera.

He surfaced, and for a worried moment, he couldn't find Milan. But in the next instant, the thief was right next to him. And they were each riding their own kelpie.

Algernon was seated on a being actually made up of water!

It shouldn't have been possible—water shouldn't be solid. He ought to have fallen into the waves and drowned. And that was what kelpies were supposed to do: they drowned their victims and maybe even ate them.

"Hold on!" Vicky shouted.

She raised her sword like a warrior about to lead a charge, and they were off.

Algernon grabbed the kelpie's very solid mane and tightened his legs on the horse.

Their three kelpies were joined by a herd of others, and Algernon let out a whoop of joy.

At his side, he heard Vicky start to laugh and Milan yell, "Amazing!"

The kelpies moved so fast that the wind against Algernon's face felt solid, and the sea itself—when he made the mistake of looking down—was a blur.

When they reached land a few moments later, the kelpies stopped abruptly.

Algernon couldn't resist petting the side of the water horse's neck. "That was brilliant. Thank you."

The kelpie twisted its neck around, and for a moment, Algernon thought it might bite him—until he realized that it was smiling.

All the kelpies made a bucking motion, lifting their back ends high enough that it seemed that they were doing handstands on their front hooves, and the three kids were tossed into the city street.

"Oof!" Milan said as he rolled onto his back beside Algernon.

Vicky looked down at them. She had obviously rolled to her feet upon landing. Her sword was still in hand.

Milan bounded to his feet and held a hand out to Algernon, who took it gratefully. He checked his pocket for the jar of medicine Ebba had offered Vicky. It was unbreakable, but it could fall out of a pocket.

"It's there," he told Vicky, holding it up.

She nodded, but she didn't reach for it. "Hold on to it for me."

"Do you know where we're going?" Milan asked.

Vicky pointed to the edge of the spire of the Glass Castle and grinned before saying, "Found it."

Algernon grinned back at her. He knew that scary things were in their future—today and later. But so far, they had survived today—and what a strange, exhilarating day it was! That was worth a smile or two.

CHAPTER 42

Vicky

The walk through the city seemed to somehow take forever and not enough time all at once. Vicky didn't even hide her sword, despite the looks she received. She felt better with it in her hand.

Vicky glanced at the ground, and her shadow was partly there. It wasn't dark, like shadows usually were, but it was a hazy grayish thing on the ground.

Algernon and Milan looked at it, too.

"You *were* kind of creepy without it," Milan said. "Still your friend and all, but I'm glad you're going to be more normal now."

"I was not creepy," Vicky insisted. She looked at Algernon and asked, "Was I?"

"Not as much as Ebba," Algernon said mildly, and Vicky couldn't help but chuckle.

"This feelings-coming-back thing is confusing," she muttered.

As they approached the castle, Vicky was grateful that she didn't have all of her feelings back just yet. She felt braver than normal—but maybe that was due to knowing her sisters were alive or having Milan and Algernon at her side.

"I'm here to see the queen," she announced. After a pause, she added, "Please let her know that her cousin, Victoria Wardrop, is here."

Behind her, she heard Algernon make a pained noise and Milan swallow a laugh.

The guards stared at her.

"My mother, Lady Wardrop, was her personal guard," Vicky explained.

"You're *Kat's* kid?" the oldest guard asked.

"And Wilbur's," Vicky added. "*He* was a Raven, too." Then she pointed at Algernon. "This is her future chief poisoner."

"Alchemist," Algernon quickly corrected. "I'm her next *alchemist.*"

"And him?" another guard asked.

"I'm Milan." He grinned. "The queen *invited* me to visit."

Vicky watched the guards and waited. She silently used her sword to pull ley line energy and draw a ward of protection around her friends—just in case.

The oldest guard sighed. "Come on, then."

Another one met Vicky's gaze and muttered, "You remind me of your mother, but more brash. She *never* went around telling people she was related to the queen."

"Yes," Vicky said agreeably. "But people found out, didn't they? And now she's dead."

The guard softened. "Your parents were good people."

Vicky nodded, grateful that most of her grief was still locked away, and motioned him forward.

The guards led them through the castle, and in a few minutes, they were walking into the throne room.

Unlike the first time Vicky had been here, the queen was alone. Their footsteps echoed in the giant room as Vicky and her friends approached.

"Younger Nightshade," the queen said. "Thief."

The boys bowed.

Vicky did not curtsy or bow. She simply drew her sword and asked, "I'd like to know why my family was killed."

The Glass Queen looked her up and down, her gaze lingering on the sword in Vicky's grasp. "I allowed you to keep that, Victoria."

"I doubt the guards could've taken it," Vicky said. "It's an athame, too. I believe *you* have the other one like it. Swords and wards, the royal skills . . ."

The Glass Queen smiled. "So you *do* realize that you are my heir, my only living relative."

"I don't want to be royal," Vicky blurted out. "I just need to know why my parents were murdered. Did you order it?"

"Will you believe me if I say no?" the queen asked. "Because I *didn't* do it. I went through the loss of my own family. Your mother was all I had left. You must know I would never put you through what we went through."

"I'm not sure I can believe you," Vicky admitted.

Queen Evangeline folded her hands together and met Vicky's gaze. "I want you to know that I protected your mother for years. Hid her away with the most reliable people I could find—where no one would think to seek her."

"With thieves," Milan said quietly.

"Yes, thieves. They have a code of honor I respect," the queen said. "And the thieves in my city are rarely arrested, because of my debt to them. The best become Ravens, but that's another story."

"I want to hear that one sometime," Milan said eagerly.

"In time." The queen smiled at him, then turned back to Vicky. "I tried to keep your family here, where they'd be safe, but your mother was stubborn. I tried to get you and your older sister sent to Corvus, where you'd best learn how to protect yourselves."

"My mother didn't trust you."

"True."

"Neither does Ebba," Algernon added.

"The chimera is angry with me, but I'd like to be on good terms with them."

"I think this would help." Algernon removed the jar and walked toward her. "This is from Ebba," he said. "This Nightshade is happy to serve the queen."

"And swear on your throne that it wasn't you that ordered the death of my family," Vicky said.

"All right," the Glass Queen said. She opened the jar and scooped some of the antidote into her hand. Her other hand tightened on a large jewel in the side of her throne as she swallowed it.

Then the Glass Queen stood and drew a sword that had been hidden inside the throne itself. "I swear on my throne that I did not murder or order the murder of my only living relatives."

Hearing these words, Vicky let out a huge sigh of relief.

The queen dropped her head, and in that moment, she looked much smaller than she had before. "I tried to protect her," she whispered. "And now she's dead . . . They're all dead. You and I are the only survivors, Victoria. And we have no choice but to serve the empire," the queen added.

"But . . ."

The queen lifted her head and made a gesture that opened every door and window in the throne room. As guards and Ravens poured into the room, the queen's voice rang out loud and clear, "I summon you here—upon advice from my network of *trusted* Ravens—to witness this long-awaited declaration. I now declare Victoria Wardrop, daughter of Kathleen and Wilbur, as my heir."

The queen looked around the room.

"I give you Victoria Wardrop, my cousin. My heir. Your future queen."

Vicky gazed at the crowd of guards and Ravens and officials as they all kneeled.

Near the front of the crowd, she saw Master Nightshade and Meister Tik and the headmaster. The headmaster scowled, but the other two men were beaming. Meredith was also there, looking happy, too.

"With her," the queen continued, "are her future advisor and alchemist, Sir Milan Glass and the young Master Nightshade, and the heir's personal guard, Lady Meredith Ward."

Merry stepped in front of Vicky and curtsied to the queen and then to Vicky. "I will protect your heir with my life, as another thief once protected you, Your Majesty."

A wave of surprise washed over Vicky, leaving her speechless. Next, Rupert and Uncle Millicent flew into the room.

"Tell Ebba," the queen said to them before looking pointedly at Nightshade.

Then the queen continued, her voice as steady as if she had not been on the verge of tears only a moment ago. "The children will continue to attend Corvus, Headmaster Edwards."

"Your Majesty," the headmaster said, bowing even deeper.

"Cousin? Your Majesty?" Vicky interrupted.

The queen looked at her.

"I would like to request that the headmaster be removed from Corvus," Vicky said.

The crowd erupted, and the headmaster took a step toward Vicky.

The queen lifted one hand. He stopped—and the room fell silent.

"Why is that, Victoria?"

"My family . . . *Your* family . . . Our families," Vicky said shakily, "were murdered. Years ago, when you were young, and now recently. And my parents warned me not to trust him."

"She's a *child*." The headmaster stared down at her. "Evangeline—"

"*Queen* Evangeline," Meister Tik interrupted, joining them.

"The chimera *really* doesn't trust him," Algernon blurted out, earning a grin from his father. Then he turned to the queen. "They think your advisors are misleading you—not that *you* are at fault, Your Majesty."

"Are you suggesting that you spoke to that *creature*?" the headmaster asked. "There are laws."

"Laws that *you* suggested, Horatio." The queen stepped toward Vicky. "Yes, so you spoke to Ebba?"

"We did," Vicky said. Milan and Algernon nodded.

"And the headmaster lied to me," Vicky added. "He tried to get me to leave Corvus with him. He *said* you wanted to see me."

The queen stared at Headmaster Edwards. "That *is* a lie. I did not summon the child."

"Meister Tik and Master Nightshade guessed that," Vicky added.

Then the seemingly distracted Master Nightshade looked up and spoke. "Ebba is wise. Three heads, you know. Chimeras are clever."

Vicky and the queen exchanged a look. "Would you feel safer, cousin, if Horatio were not at Corvus?"

"I would." Vicky took a big gulp of air and added, "But not if it meant he was too near *you*."

The queen paused and smiled. Then she made a gesture.

Guards took the headmaster's arms. He called out, "Penelope! Agatha!"

Neither ward mistress nor dragon appeared to help him.

"This is absurd," he yelled.

"An investigation might be wise," Meister Tik said to the queen.

She nodded and touched his shoulder in a way that reminded Vicky of her parents. Then Queen Evangeline said, "Mind the school for me, Tik. I want only loyal Ravens."

They did whatever weird thing grown-ups did when they

stared in each other's eyes in silence, and then Meister Tik bowed to the queen. He hadn't been there to see her take the antidote, but he knew somehow.

"I expect great things of you, cousin," the queen said warmly. She pulled Vicky in for a hug.

A hug.

Of all the weird things that had happened, the queen hugging her seemed the strangest.

And then the queen was gone. Vicky wished she could tell her parents that the queen had been tricked, that she hadn't turned against her family. Most of all, she wished she could ask them if she was making the right choice.

"Ripples, Princess," Rupert said. "They all add up to change."

"Kat would be pleased. Ebba will be, too," Uncle Millicent said before he flew out of the room.

Vicky stood there. She hadn't fought with swords or wards. She hadn't needed to get rid of her feelings. She'd still done scary things—stood up to adults in power, decided whom to trust, and asked hard questions.

Ripples, she thought.

"That went better than expected," Algernon said from her right side.

"Or worse," Milan added from her left.

"Yes," Vicky said. "It really did, didn't it?"

But now she had to figure out school, and friends, and family—and being a princess. That was all scary, too.

Meredith announced, "Clear the room. The heir needs space."

Vicky hadn't meant to end up as the future queen, and she wasn't sure she wanted that, but she was feeling hopeful. Life. Safety. Freedom. A home. At least some of it was possible.

"We're at your side," Algernon reminded her.

"Literally," Milan added with a smirk.

"And I'm at yours," Vicky said. "Friends. Together, we'll figure this out."

She smiled, took her friends' hands, and with Merry clearing a path, they made their way out the door and into Glass City.

EPILOGUE

◆————————◆————————◆

Rupert watched them walk out the door and into Glass City. Small though they were now, these children were strong of heart and will. They'd cured the Glass Queen. They'd stood up to power. They'd created more ripples of change.

As the gargoyle flew outside, the crowd parted for the small girl with a sword, the boy with the scent of *home* on him, and the other boy and girl with the ferocity of young dragonets and the quick hands of faeries.

"Gots to go. Move, move, move!" The dragonet called Penelope went zipping by. "Pen'lpee stay with Milan and thems now . . ."

"Creatures of both worlds working together," Nightshade said, sounding both pleased and shocked.

"As it should be," Rupert said, settling his stony feathers. He had spent what, to him, was a blink of time here, and change was happening.

He saw it in the human queen's eyes, tears filling them as her feelings returned. He saw it in the dragonet-like Merry, who was ready to raise wards or swords for Vicky Love. And he knew Ebba felt it, because the chimera had sent kelpies to ferry the children to the city.

"Rupert?" Tik moved through the crowd, trailing Nightshade.

"She's doing what Kat started," Rupert said. "Minor Nightshade is, too. And the others."

"Facing a *chimera*, though?" Tik frowned.

"Well, Ebba has a good heart or three," Rupert said. "And now the Glass Queen has one, too. Hearts matter."

Tik and Nightshade stood at Rupert's sides, worrying. "These are good ripples," the gargoyle assured them.

"They'll need lessons," Tik said.

"And tinctures," Nightshade added.

Rupert leaned against first Tik and then Nightshade. "And family."

Much as Rupert had needed when he first came through the door and met them. Much as he still did. They weren't nestmates, these featherless creatures, but they were *his*— and he had grown to love them. Their willpower, their integrity, their generosity.

No, they were not defenseless, these creatures. Small acts of love, of loyalty, of justice were adding up. Good would continue to grow and make more of itself. Like ripples. A small act flowed into a towering wave—and that was true in any world.

ACKNOWLEDGMENTS

I am usually terse with these, but this book is a decade in the making. Please feel free to not read this, but I must thank a longer than usual list of people.

My sidekick-in-research deserves a big portion of gratitude. In 2014, we spent several weeks in Europe celebrating my daughter's high school graduation—and researching this book. So thank you, Asia, for accompanying me to random cities for world-building. It's been a long time between then and now, so I suppose we will need a trip to celebrate your PhD upon this book's release. (We shan't discuss the weird truth that you got two degrees during the gestation and publication of this novel!)

Thank you, Dylan, for agreeing to take that first mother-son sword-fighting class—and being willing to hit your mother with a sword. Thank you, also, for not continuing to want to go away to boarding school. The research informed this book—"houses" for different groups and the like—but my life is better because you didn't move away.

Thank you, Neil, for Scottish hospitality.

Thank you, Amy, for French hospitality.

Thank you, Youval, for Dutch hospitality.

Thank you to Sunny at the Avantgarde Prague for Czech insights, warnings, and wisdom.

Thank you to the staff at the Speculum Alchemiae for answering so many questions after my tour of the alchemy museum.

Thank you to Bill Grandy, Dagi, and the staff at the Virginia Academy of Fencing. Coach Bill, it remains a joy and pleasure to have been your student in sword and in the history of the sword. You are, quite truly, an inspiration, and it is an honor to know you.

Thank you to Esfinges. The "give a girl a sword" sentiment is brilliant; hopefully, my book will spark that dream, too.

Thank you, Kim Salzano at Pilates Harmony in Virginia; Valya at Power Pilates in Virginia; and Viviane at Vivit Pilates in Delft, Netherlands. You kept me strong enough to recover from surgeries.

Thanks to Vanessa and Christine at Function Pilates in Arizona. Because of you, I recovered from both a stroke and a rattlesnake bite.

Thank you, Mesa Public Library and Tempe Public Library, for hosting my Swordfighting for Women classes. It was a joy to "give a woman a sword," and your space made that possible.

Thank you, Brennan, for telling me that you wanted gender-fluid characters in kidlit. The chimera exists because of our conversations. It has been a joy to know you both in your childhood and adulthood.

Thank you, Meghan, for being the kind of sister you are to B. You, Brennan, and my own kids were the inspiration for the strong sibling bonds in this book.

Thank you, Kelley and all of the writers who joined me on retreats to revise this over and over for all these years.

Thank you, Merrilee, for patience even when we disagree and for loving my weird fantasy book.

Thank you, Laura, Jeanette, and Asia, for reading draft after draft.

Thank you to Kelley and Jeaniene for loving me enough to pull me out of my "I'm going to quit writing!" state. Your support during my sick years was everything.

Thank you, Amber, for waking my heart.

Thank you to Charles Marr, who was here when I began this book back in 2011 and gone from my life too soon. Uncle Charles, this Victorian love of mine was yours first. Many of these characters have a touch of your DNA. Uncle Albert's stiff facade and Master Nightshade's forgetfulness and clutter are written with fondness because they are the traits of a loving uncle. I miss you. I miss our "secret language." No one writes to me in quotes, crafting literary puzzles to which I must reply. Should my words reach the other side, I say to you: "'What heart heard of, ghost guessed.' Mortality is a horrid thing."

And thank you, Nancy Paulsen, for seeing what I was trying to say. Sometimes that gift is the rarest of finds. And like the children in my story, I figured out where I needed to be thanks in large part to your wisdom.